MONTOBA

THE PRINCESS OF ÉLEVÉ

A NOVEL

AN HISTORICAL FANTASY

ED STRUM

Acknowledgements

Many thanks to Leslie Brown, Heather Couthaud and Jim Jacobs for reviewing the novel numerous times and suggesting various editing changes. My appreciation also to Sandra Geist, Brad Strum, Graham Crawbuck, Tyler Strum and Trevor Strum.

MONTOBA

Books by Ed Strum

THE CONNOISSSEURS – A Play

MONTOBA: THE PRINCESS OF ÉLEVÉ – A Novel

THE BURROW – A Play

JOURNEY OF THE SCROLLS – A Novel

JOURNEY OF THE SCROLLS – SPECIAL EDITION

THE PRINCESS OF ÉLEVÉ – A Play

EVERY DAY IS A GOOD DAY – A Play

THE HOLLOW PENCIL – A Play

CASCADIA and THE GREAT PANDEMIC – A Novel

ADAM'S ARK & THE GREAT PANDEMIC – A Play

RICHIE – A Poetic Play in One Scene

A SENSORY FEAST – An Anthology of Prose Poetry

CONTENTS

Appendices

PROLOGUE

Captive

Princess Mia woke up slowly from a long sleep to the sound of the gurgling stream which trickled through a corner of her confined space. She had no idea how long she'd been sleeping. All she knew was that she was in a dark place, a deep cave, and that the entrance was blocked. She could see a sliver of light from a small crack piercing the darkness surrounding her. She was trapped but was thankful she still had her little back pack with a small amount of food. Where was she? Who captured her? Why was she being held captive? And how long would she languish in this dank, uncomfortable cave?

She reasoned that someone or some creature must have captured her for some sinister reason. Why didn't they kill her? Did they know who she was? Did they plan to ransom her if they knew her identity? Or did they plan to sell her as a slave, or worse? She shuddered at the possibilities and tried to push these thoughts from her mind.

If only she had some means to communicate with her friend Pre, he would surely come to rescue her. How long would it take him to realize she was not returning, and to mount an attempt to find her? She could only wait, and wait. And sleep! She had plenty of time to do that. There was nothing else she could do.

ONE

Discovering the Tablets
Southeast Asia – Island of Sumatra, Summer, 2036

Archie stopped her digging, put her shovel down, and cocked her head. She heard only the soft murmur of a light breeze sliding down the steep cliffs. Far below she could make out the small figures of her party moving through the valley. She took off her helmet and wiped the sweat and dirt from her face. Her strawberry blonde hair tumbled down below her shoulders.

Archie was seventeen and about to enter her first year at Yale. Seventeen! Like the seventeen syllables in haiku, arranged neatly. *Ah, but the best years are yet to come,* she thought. It was the end of the hot Indonesian summer. Archie and a team of student archaeologists had come with their faculty adviser Andre to search this site for ancient artifacts. It was thought there'd been a very early civilization here and the artifacts would provide proof. Andre had been given permission to search an area in northwest Sumatra covering many kilometers around a huge lake. The lake was one hundred kilometers long and thirty kilometers wide, and had an island in the middle.

The war on the island of Borneo, they were told, might spread to neighboring islands, and Andre's team should expect trouble. *They need not have worried*, mused Archie. The trip had so far proven to be uneventful and summer was coming to an end in a few days.

Archie had climbed to the ridge high above the rest of the team where she had been digging for several minutes. The ridge was part of a ring of mountains that surrounded the lake. She knew the cliffs also dropped rapidly on the other side into the lake. She wondered if she might be at the same altitude as the lake.

The idea occurred to her that it would be so convenient to have a tunnel that went through the mountain range. She smiled to herself and thought, *I should be so lucky to find such a passageway if it existed.* A shiver went down her spine. She had a strange feeling she was about to find something, something very important. But what? And where?

She had been drawn to this spot by what looked like a great gray owl, but even larger. She had only seen a great gray once before, in the mountains of the Sierras, back in the States. It resembled a giant moth. As she followed this "giant moth", which circled above, her hazel eyes were drawn to this area that was different than the rest of the cliff face.

It was an indentation into the steep cliff and had a more gradual slope. Instead of the rocky surface, she noticed this area of the cliff was composed of loose ash colored dirt, but darker than the surrounding rock. It had recently been exposed, she felt, but from what? Was it from rain and wind, or maybe a recent earthquake?

The darker color narrowed to an arch and abruptly stopped. Below the arch it looked just like a doorway that had been covered with dirt and ash. She resumed her digging, and with a few more shovelfuls and a hard push, the ground gave way and she fell forward into the opening.

The smell from the opening caused her to pull back. It was stale, dry, and dusty, and suffocating. The outside air gradually replaced the lifeless and oppressive air inside. When she could breathe again, she dug a hole about two feet in diameter, and stepped in. She lost her balance and tumbled and rolled downward some twenty or twenty-five meters. She stopped at a hard rock wall.

Aside from having the breath knocked out of her, she was unhurt. She reached in her backpack for her torchlight and turned it on. *Thank heavens*, she thought, *it wasn't broken in the fall*. She moved her light around. She found her helmet, put it on, and tucked her long blonde hair inside.

She noticed that ash spread below the opening, and that she was in a tunnel rather than a cave. She moved down the passageway twenty meters and looked at the smooth rocky walls. Perhaps they'd been carved by underground rivers but there was no evidence of rivers or water nearby. *I'd better let Andre know where I am*, she thought, *before I go any farther*.

She climbed back to the entrance and heard yelling. It was Yuri! He had followed her. She was glad to hear his voice. Archie had met him at the start of summer and immediately liked him. He was different than the others. He was sweet. He was funny. His long black hair came down to his shoulders and his dark brown eyes looked deeply into her own. He made her feel good when she was with him. She felt much safer exploring this area with Yuri around. At six feet he was half a foot taller than Archie. He wasn't afraid of anything. He was like the brother she always wanted but never had.

"Archie!" He ran effortlessly up the hill as he called, "Archie, where've you been? I've been worried you got lost. I thought I saw you start climbing but then I looked up and you'd disappeared. What are you up to?"

"Look, Yuri," she motioned him to follow her, "look what I found. I need your help." Archie turned back to the entrance of the tunnel and showed Yuri the small opening.

"Wow," he said, "Where does it go?" Yuri looked inside with the light. "It goes almost straight down."

"Yes, I know," she replied, "I want to explore it further. Hold this. Give a tug if someone comes."

Archie gave Yuri one end of a thin rope. She unrolled the rope as she descended. After about two hundred meters of descent, she found herself in

3

an open cavern, six or seven meters in diameter. The passageway continued on the other side of the cavern.

This was definitely man made, she thought. The floor was covered with rocks that had fallen from above and cracks ran in all directions. It was as if some monster had shaken everything violently. *An earthquake?*

She noticed there were several crevices on the sides of the walls partly filled with dirt. She took her pickax and probed. There was a clank as if she had hit some kind of metal. She peered in with her light, and saw a tiny glint from something shiny lodged in the crevice. She reached in and gently removed it, dusting off the dirt and ash.

It was shaped like one of the notebook computers they used decades before, about the size of a book. She noticed it was a set of tablets, as if pages in a book, very thin tablets. They were so very light in her hand, amazingly light, and yet appeared to be made of a type of metal. But how could they be so light?

She opened a tablet "page" carefully and looked closely at the fine markings, or engravings, on it. She used her magnifying glass to look at the markings. *Astounding* she thought. They appeared to be regular repeating patterns.

"Archie! Where are you?" She felt a tug on the rope. She wrapped the tablets in a shirt and put them in her backpack.

"I'm coming," she yelled. Her heart was pounding. She hurried up to the entrance. "What is it, Yuri?"

"It's Andre," Yuri said. "He wants us to meet at our rendezvous spot in two hours. What shall I tell him?"

Neither of them moved.

"Tell him we're at the cliffs half way up, and we'll meet at the rendezvous spot on time." Yuri repeated her words.

"Alright, Archie, what's going on?" he asked.

"Tie the rope to that tree and come with me," she replied. She led him down to the cavern. She pointed to the tunnel on the other side of the cavern. "We still have enough rope left for several hundred meters. Follow me."

Yuri drew an imaginary sword and waved it in the air. "Whatever you are, prepare to die." He charged into the passageway holding his light in the other hand. Archie struggled to keep up. The tunnel continued downwards two hundred meters and opened into a wide, open cavern.

Archie was drawn to one large crevice along the edge of the floor. She used her pickax to pry the rocks away and heard the sound of her ax hitting metal. She pulled out a small light box made of the same material as her tablets.

"Yuri!" she whispered. "Take it." Yuri took the box and held it in his hand. He pried it open. His eyes became as large as an owl's eyes in the dim light of her torch.

4

"Mon dieu!" he spoke softly. He picked up a small glittering object. "Archie, these are diamonds. This is one of the most beautiful I've ever seen. Flawless. And cut beautifully. Who could have done this? Do you realize what we've found?" They looked silently at each other.

"Yuri, are you sure?" Archie whispered in awe.

"Absolutely, Archie. This is exquisite!"

She looked in the box. There were several dozen, of all sizes and different cuts. They glistened even in the dim light. He was right. They were beautiful. Archie shivered. And then she noticed a small hand carved wooden tool in the box that looked as if it was for measuring.

Who put it there? When? Who did the diamonds belong to? They'd obviously been hidden for safekeeping. Why?

"Yuri, we shouldn't take them," she blurted out, "they don't belong to us. Put them back. We can get them later."

Yuri hesitated and reluctantly put the box back in the crevice and concealed it with small rocks. He peered further into the passageway to see what lay before.

"Archie, we can't go any further. We must start back." Yuri was quiet. "We promised Andre we'd meet at the rendezvous spot. We have just enough time."

Archie nodded. She turned and climbed slowly up the passegeway back to the opening. Yuri followed closely behind. They moved away from the opening and started down the hill. Archie suddenly stopped.

"Yuri, I need to tell Andre about the passageway."

"Andre," she called on the radio, "we found a tunnel."

"Archie!" He yelled on the radio. *"I've been calling. Where have you been? We have to leave immediately."*

"We found an opening to a passageway in the side of the cliff. It goes down into...," she blurted out, but was interrupted by Andre.

"Archie, never mind about that now. Is Yuri with you?" Andre was abrupt. Something must have happened.

"Yes. Is something wrong?" she responded quietly.

"We must evacuate immediately," Andre yelled. "We can't stay longer. Get to the jet helicopter immediately."

"Alright. We're on our way," she answered softly.

"Archie?" Andre's voice softened.

"Yes? I'm still here," she replied evenly.

"Archie, I'm sorry I yelled. The tunnel you say you found? It's probably caused by an underground river from centuries ago, but note the surroundings and leave some sort of mark near the location anyway. We'll check it out when we come back. But hurry. We have very little time."

5

"Alright, we'll get there as fast as we can." She had tried to tell him, she reasoned. It would come up later.

Archie and Yuri carried unusual stones to the entrance to mark the spot. She noted the GPS readings. *No one is going to find this while I'm gone,* she reflected, *if I can help it!*

The battle sounds came from the south. *This fighting's been going on for years,* she mused, *when will it end?*

As they sped to Singapore, she told Andre about the tunnel and caverns. She was puzzled that Andre was only mildly interested and decided it was the turn of events that distracted him.

Archie reflected back to their briefing.

"The cliffs we will explore are the rim of a super volcano. The lake is the caldera remaining after the occurrence of a cataclysmic explosion seventy five thousand years ago," Andre had said, then had reviewed the scientific evidence. Scientists from different disciplines had come to the conclusion that mankind almost became extinct then, most certainly from this catastrophic event. All living creatures above the ground for thousands of miles around had died.

The evidence pointed to one place and one point in time. If mankind had come close to the brink of extinction, what evidence could they find about those that had lived in this area? How far-reaching was the devastation? How close to extinction had mankind come? What had saved them? How many people had survived and why? Where had they gone?

Archie and Yuri sat next to each other on the flight to the US, in silence. She had told no one of her discovery of the tablets. They were wrapped up carefully in her luggage.

"Yuri?" Archie startled him. "What are you thinking?"

"Oh, just about the tunnels. Wondering where they go." He stared into her eyes. His gaze was intense. "Archie?"

"Yes, what?" She waited for him to continue.

"Remember when I put the box of diamonds back?"

"Yes. Why?"

"I didn't put back the diamond I took out of the box," he went on, "I don't know what came over me. I must have put it in my pocket without even thinking. It's in my baggage with the other rocks I picked up."

She felt a wave of relief and put her arms around Yuri.

"Oh, Yuri! I'm so glad." He looked at her with amazement. "What I mean is we have something to show Andre. And the team. We can find out how old it is with radiocarbon dating tests."

He shook his head slowly. "Archie, no we can't! We should've brought the box back after all."

She was puzzled. "What are you talking about?"

6

"We could have left the diamonds there but we needed the box. You can't do radiocarbon testing on diamonds to tell their age." He let that sink in. "But you could on the contents. You test on organic carbon like that wooden tool. I don't know what came over me. I wasn't thinking."

"You were under a spell," she laughed. She gave him another hug. "It's alright, Yuri." Archie would tell Yuri about the tablets but now she needed sleep. She hadn't slept for over twenty-four hours. She drifted off, her mind playing with the seventeen syllables of her poem in the form of a haiku.

Carboniferous
Hieroglyphic mystery
Antiquity runes.

TWO

Deciphering the Tablets; Magic Wafers; an Object in Space
Yale University - January, 2037

Two days after the start of the school year, Andre asked to see Archie and Yuri, to conduct a "debriefing".

"Archie, you went down several hundred meters?"

"Yes, over four hundred, I'd say," Archie responded.

"And found it blocked then?"

"Yes."

"There were two caverns?"

"Yes, very wide, perhaps six or seven meters wide."

"Were they natural? Or man made?" He stared intently.

"Man made." That was all. He asked no more questions.

"Archie?" Yuri stared at her. She understood.

"Andre," Archie said, "Yuri and I have more to tell you about our discoveries." She told Andre about the box of diamonds, and apologized for not bringing any back.

"I felt they didn't belong to us. Later I realized how valuable the contents were. They could be dated. I'm sorry."

"Do you think you could find the box again?"

"I'm sure of it." She was surprised at her confidence.

Andre was clearly disappointed. He thanked Archie.

"I guess we'll just have to be resigned to the situation."

It was then she dropped her bombshell. As Andre made a small motion to get up from his chair, she stopped him.

"Wait! I have something to show both of you."

She pulled the tablets from her backpack. Yuri's eyes opened wide. Andre's face showed joy and relief.

Andre and Yuri started talking with rising voices, overlapping each other, about how important this was to the team. They calmed down, looked at the book of tablets, and opened the pages. Andre held the tablets up in front of him.

"Would it be alright if we put this under lock and key?" he asked Archie. "You'll still have access to it."

She could not object to this safeguard.

"But first I'll ask the lab to do radiocarbon dating on it."

The lab found an insect, a small leaf and human hair between the pages. They also used a leather strip separating two pages for radiocarbon dating, and an attached bone used in the original binding.

Archie and Andre agreed not to discuss the tablets or the box until Andre explored the legalities with the university. Archie was allowed to study the tablets, which were kept in the library. For hours, she sat there deciphering the tablets, and soon began to see repetitions and distinct patterns. She worked through the holidays knowing she might have little time before she had to stop. Her work paid off. She had succeeded in translating important sections and wanted to show Yuri her results.

It was the first day of classes in the New Year and Archie had just finished her last class. Archie left the School of Architecture and headed for her room in Timothy Dwight. She had to cross the entire campus to get to her room but she didn't mind. She felt the cold biting wind and snow on her cheeks but she didn't mind that either. She looked up at Yuri's window in Branford. It was dark inside. He wasn't back yet from his trip but he was due to arrive. She went directly to her room knowing he would go there first. She had so much to tell him. "Oh, Yuri," she murmured to herself, "I've missed you a lot."

"I'm so happy to be at Yale," Archie said softly, "I feel so much at home here." She shook the snow off her cloak, took it off, and hung it up to dry, then dropped her backpack, and sat down. She was so glad she had bought her "chamy", her chamelame suit. It fit like a glove and was so light and flexible, and warm. She wondered who had invented it.

She turned on a lamp, pulled out her notebook, and put it on the table. She reached into a side pocket of her backpack and pulled out her handkerchief which was shaped in a ball. She opened the handkerchief and took out four wafers the size of quarters. She placed them on the table. She looked at them through her glass and made notes in her journal.

There was a knock at the door. Archie wrapped the wafers in the handkerchief and put them back in her pack. Yuri came in the open door. He dropped his suitcase.

"Archie, are you here?" he called. She heard him take his backpack off and unbutton his coat.

"In here, Yuri," she yelled. Yuri rushed in to her room, tossed his backpack down, and put his arms around her. "Oh, Yuri! I've missed you so much." She lingered in his strong arms. He felt so warm. Finally she pulled away and let him take off his coat. "How was your trip?"

"It was terrific until I presented my paper." Yuri slumped into a chair. She put her arm around his shoulders.

"I'm sorry."

"Scientists aren't as open-minded as you might think, especially when their beliefs are challenged. But I want to hear all about the tablets. How's it coming? Finished yet?"

"Almost."

Archie's mind drifted back to her recent work. She'd made marvelous progress but she was running out of time. Then she'd made the discovery of the wafers! She'd been turning the tablet sheets, the "pages", which were clearly meant to be looked at like a book. Hidden in a pocket created within several sheets together were four thin gray wafers. She did something she'd normally never do: smuggle the wafers out of the library. Her hands had shaken when she locked up the tablets, without the wafers. *I'm getting pretty good at smuggling things,* she mused.

"Archie!" Yuri startled her. "You drifted off, sort of spaced out. Are you alright?"

"I'm sorry, Yuri. I was thinking," she continued, "I've translated much of the journal while you were gone. I'll show you. But first I have to show you something else."

Archie took the handkerchief with the four wafers from her backpack, opened it, and showed him the wafers.

"What are they?" He looked at her expectantly.

"I found them hidden in the pages of the tablets."

"Do you know what they are?" He looked puzzled.

"Not yet," she lied. She put the wafers on the table. "I'm looking for some reference to them." Archie felt it was not the time to tell Yuri. He wouldn't believe her. "Look," she directed him to her notes, "this language is based on sounds, like phonemes."

"That makes sense to me. Most ancient languages were passed on by the spoken word. They didn't write anything down. So then why is **this** language written down?"

"But that's the point. Whoever decided to write all this down did so to pass on a description of their world. That's the only explanation I can come up with."

"How do you know what it means?"

"That's the neat thing. The writer added little pictures of objects, to help me understand what the markings mean." She wasn't ready to tell Yuri that the pictures included creatures she'd never seen before, and what appeared to be riddles.

"Isn't that like the Mayan hieroglyphs? The ones they analyzed in the middle of the last century?"

"Exactly! They were phonetic also. They had a picture-image, called a rebus, and a symbol, a logogram, next to the phonetic hieroglyphs. It's almost the same with these."

"Archie, you think you were meant to find the tablets?"

"Whoever wrote the tablets wanted **someone** to find them, but what do they expect me to do?"

"Archie, did you get the radiocarbon dating tests back yet? Have you found out how old the tablets are?"

"The tests should arrive today. They're doing them up the hill in the lab. They said they'd drop off a copy to me on their way to give the results to Andre."

"Yuri, there's something strange. The writing changes part way through, as if another person took it over. The first one talks of their advanced technology. Read this!" As he read out loud, Yuri's voice slowed and his eyes grew wider.

"There once was a great city called Montoba. The city surrounded a huge mountain, and towered one kilometer into the air. Tunnels and caverns extended the underground part of the city ten kilometers below the surface.

The city received its energy from a solar energy system that collected sunlight for over one hundred kilometers in all directions and concentrated it into the upper parts of the tall towers and then down into the city reservoirs of energy. The city also received heat from boiling thermal fountains and rivers, and tapped into the intense temperatures just outside of the superheated magma chamber."

"So what do you think of that?" Archie queried. "Astounding, isn't it? One kilometer into the air. Yuri, remember that Japanese skyscraper project? The one where they were planning to build a mile high building? They never built it, did they? But in ancient times they did."

"Come on, Archie. An ancient civilization, technologically advanced, even more than ours?"

"Well, it's possible. Look at how advanced the civilizations were in Egypt, in Greece, and in Rome? We still can't duplicate Egyptian technology."

"Yes, but at least we've known about them for a long time. You think this civilization was much older?"

"Yuri, read on. There's more. It becomes ominous. It's the second writer." She put the notebook in front of him.

"The city is in ruins. The three tribes fought wars that destroyed the city. The remaining people were threatened by wild creatures, strange clouds that kill, and the towering mountain. The dangers have pushed most living creatures, including humans, to the brink of extinction."

He jumped up. "Archie! A civilization that we didn't know existed? That became extinct?" Archie was quiet.

"It's possible. Yuri, you don't believe me?"

"Come on! Someone's playing a hoax. The tablets and box can't be more than a couple of hundred years old."

"No, Yuri. The tablets talk about the diamonds they use to write the tablets. I need to solve the riddle and…"

"Riddle? What riddle?" His tone was sharp.

"One in particular refers to a hidden treasure, but it's vague as to where it's located. It's obscure on purpose."

"Come on, Archie. Be real…."

"Yuri, I didn't want to tell you. I know what the tablets say about the wafers. They transport you back in time."

Yuri held up his hands. He snapped at her.

"This is too much. Archie, don't you recognize a big hoax when you see it? Ancient extinct civilizations? Riddles? Hidden treasure? And now magic wafers?"

She'd had enough and snarled at Yuri.

"No more than you. Aren't you imagining this meteor you're tracking is jumping around? I'm sorry, Yuri."

"They're all skeptical. It's against all known evidence. Archie, I'm not imagining this. Look!" He pulled out a stack of time lapse photos. "These show its direction.Then it goes in a different direction. It's behaving erratically."

"That's not possible."

"You? A science student? You say it's not possible?"

"It must be gravitational pull from nearby objects."

"It's headed here, and honing in on us."

"How big is it? When will it get here?"

Before she said another word, there was a knock at the door. She took a letter from the courier standing there, opened it, and read it to herself. There were several pages and she read them all. She sat down, stunned. Yuri grabbed the letter from her and read the first paragraph.

"Seventy five thousand years old? Unbelievable!" He was silent. Finally he continued, "Archie, if this is true and not a hoax, explain something to me. How did these tablets last so long?"

"Yuri, read the rest. They're made of a hard substance, similar to the carbon nanotubes invented years ago. Ten times lighter than steel and 100 times stronger. They were going to build a space elevator. Remember?"

"They never did." He wasn't easily convinced. "Archie, how did the writings survive without being worn down?"

"Yuri, don't forget they've been buried all this time. They weren't exposed to air." She paused. "Yuri, do you realize there were intelligent people seventy five thousand years ago?"

"Yeah, sure. Wearing animal skins. Eating only meat. Barely surviving. But intelligent? Never!"

"Yuri, remember the studies of mitochondrial DNA? Man was close to extinction seventy five thousand years ago from a cataclysmic event, like a supervolcano. Only a few thousand people were left on the planet, scattered, probably just in Africa. There may've been only a few dozen women to reproduce. All mankind's descended from them."

"Archie, this is ridiculous. You really believe this?"

"It's possible this early civilization far surpassed our own. Everything was lost. What could've happened?"

"Archie, this is nonsense. It must be a hoax. I'll show you." Yuri was a man of action. She liked that about him. But what happened next stunned even Archie. Yuri grabbed a wafer from the table and popped it into his mouth. There was a boom, and a puff of smoke. Yuri had disappeared. Archie picked up a wafer, and looked at it, as if to figure out what had happened.

"Yuri, why did you do that?" she spoke quietly to herself. Even though she had tried to convince Yuri of the truth of what the tablets said about the wafers, she had not really believed it until it actually happened. Now it seemed to be a reality.

She shrugged and put two of the wafers in the pocket of her backpack. She noticed Yuri's backpack and picked it up. "Yuri, you may need this," she said very softly. Then she popped the remaining wafer into her mouth. There was another puff of smoke as she vanished from her room.

Booms and puffs of smoke.
Transporting magic wafers
Ancient times revealed.

THREE

In The Cavern of The Leprechaun
75000 BP (Before Present)

Yuri was stunned. He found himself alone in the middle of a large cavern, eight to ten meters across. The walls had signs that there'd previously been mining of what appeared to be slate, and on one wall there were marks that appeared to be doodles. No matter! The fact was, he'd been transported back in time just as that mysterious Indonesian tablet said. There was a large rock in front of the wall beneath the doodles, and there were steps gouged into it on one side.

He also noticed four openings in and out of the cavern, three of which appeared to be passageways. The other small one looked more like a cave since there was no foot path to it. Each tunnel had a different set of stones at the entrance. One had small stones or pebbles, another rocks of six to ten centimeters in size, and the third small boulders. A crumbling statue of a king stood near the rock entrance. The paths from the "Pebble" and "Boulder" passages crossed to the "King" one, showing a fork in the passageways.

The air in the cavern was fresh and cool as if a faint draft coursed through the passageways. Yuri decided to explore the King tunnel which appeared to be a main route. He was more curious than afraid and thought, *"Archie thinks I'm fearless. Here we go."* Withour hesitating, he dashed into the entrance.

All was silent in the underground world. Then Archie appeared in the middle of the cavern. Archie had no idea where she was, or if this was where Yuri had gone, but she wasn't surprised at all to be in some sort of cavern. After all, that was where she'd found the tablets in the first place. She stood motionless and listened. Not a sound. She made quick note of the walls, the rock, and the four openings leading out.

Yuri was nowhere to be found, but there was a faint sweet fragrance that reminded her of him. There was nothing she wanted more than to hold him again in her arms. She vowed never to argue with him if she found him.

She had a momentary thought: *perhaps he'd been transported elsewhere.* She quickly dismissed that notion. He must be nearby, she reasoned. Then she heard footsteps. Yuri came running in, out of breath, from the passage he'd been searching.

"Oh, Archie! I thought I'd blown it this time. I wasn't sure you'd come." Yuri's smile of joy filled the cavern. She ran to him with open arms.

"Yuri, what **else** could I do? I couldn't let you do this alone. It's **my** mission, my journey to take." She hugged him, "but I'm so glad to see you. I thought for a moment you'd gone somewhere else and I was on my own."

"Not a chance!" Yuri smiled and held her in his arms. "We're in this together."

She pointed to the opening from which Yuri had emerged. "Where does that go?"

"I don't know. It seems to be a tunnel. See the paths?" Yuri pointed to the paths that ran from the other passageways. "Do you really think we went back in time seventy five thousand years?"

"Look around. What do you think?" She pointed to the drawings and doodles. "See these? The same language used in my tablets. If the tablets are seventy five thousand years old, these must have also been done then. That makes sense, doesn't it?"

They were startled by a noise that sounded like snoring. They looked around but saw no one, yet the noise seemed to be close to them. They realized that the noise was coming from under the large rock below the doodles. Yuri looked under a corner of it and saw a sleeping figure.

"Look here. What's this? It's sleeping. What is it?"

Yuri's voice and movements startled the sleeper, and it woke up. It jumped up and ran into the King tunnel. It was clad all in green, with short pants, a dusty jacket, and boots.

"Why, it's a leprechaun, Yuri."

"Do your notes say anything about a leprechaun?"

"No, but that's what it looks like."

"Should I catch it? You know the legend: a leprechaun's bound to reveal the location of its treasure." Yuri started to follow him. "This is getting to be fun."

"Leave it alone," she yelled, "it looked so frightened. Don't scare it." She beckoned him to the wall. "Look at these figures and doodles." It was clear to Archie that he found the doodles less important than a real leprechaun.

"What do they say?"

"Most of it is just doodles. But there's an evil looking figure I hadn't seen before. Maybe he's after the treasure."

"Treasure? Evil figure? I can't believe it. You're such a romantic," he joked. "Maybe he's after my diamonds."

"What's this? Looks like a beetle with little arms." She stared at the wall. "It's somehow connected to the treasure."

"Beetles with arms? This is too much. Look, Archie, I don't want the leprechaun to get away. Maybe it can turn itself into a spider or something. Or a toad and hop away."

"Alright, but be gentle, will you? It seemed so terrified."

"Don't worry. I have a very gentle touch." He grinned at her and got back a smile at last.

"Don't be long," she yelled after him, "remember what the tablets said about wild creatures." She turned back to the wall looking for any reference to the treasure or beetle.

Yuri returned from the tunnel with the leprechaun walking in front of him.

"Ontde urtha ema. Ee ontwa unra ayawa," it whimpered.

"What's it saying, Yuri?"

"How should I know? Sounds like gibberish to me."

"Aaaah!" The leprechaun gave a sign of recognition when it heard their voices. It switched to their language. "Oh, you've finally come." It shook itself and brushed the dust from its ragged clothes. Its finery, green mixed with so much dust, with patches, looked like an army fatigue outfit. *His clothes must have been elegant at one time,* Archie thought, *but now the poor creature looked as if it had walked through a briar patch.* It peered at them curiously for a moment. Satisfied they wouldn't hurt him, he continued, "I said 'Don't hurt me. I won't run away.'"

"You're a leprechaun?" Archie blurted out, "and you speak our language?"

"Yes and yes. I speak all languages."

"Do you have a name, Mr. Leprechaun?" Yuri asked. "How long have you been sleeping there?"

"My name is Pre. How long have I been sleeping? Hmmm, well, that depends on what you mean. Let's just say: quite a long time." Yuri was not easily put off but this creature had him baffled. He spoke to Archie softly.

"He speaks in riddles," Yuri whispered to Archie. "What shall we do with him?"

"I'll talk to him," she said to Yuri. "Check out that cave. I'll ask him what he means." Yuri wandered into the opening. Archie realized the leprechaun was no longer afraid of them and slowly becoming more trusting.

"What's the meaning of, 'You've finally come?'"

"I knew someone would eventually find the tablets. I hoped you'd come to help us."

"Help? With what?"

"The **quest**! The **search**! I can't do it by myself."

"Yuri says you're bound to tell us where the treasure is. The one described in the tablets. Is that true?"

"I can't tell you, but I can show you, if you'll go with me. But it'll be a dangerous quest, a dangerous journey."

"Dangerous? In what way?"

"My lady, there're still some terrifying creatures left in our world, and our enemies still roam the tunnels. I could never take this long journey alone. Our legend says someday you'd come and help us. I've been waiting so long. Finally you've come."

16

Suddenly there was a cracking rumbling noise. The ground shook. Archie held her arms over her head, but the shaking stopped almost as soon as it started. *Just a small earthquake*, she thought. She'd felt a few quakes at home. She was used to them. But the leprechaun was quite alarmed by the shaking, and continued in an excited voice.

"We must go. There's no time to lose."

"It's only a little earthquake."

"It'll get worse. We must go while we still have time."

"We've **got** to wait for Yuri. He'll be right back." She grabbed Pre by the arm. "Did **you** leave the tablets?"

"I hid them years ago in a cave, not far from here. Where'd you find them?"

"Buried under soot and ash and dirt, in a crevice."

Pre nodded. "That sounds like the place I hid them."

"Why'd you hide them?"

"Just in case," he answered.

"Just in case what?" she pressed him.

"Just in case I didn't wake up," he replied. *He's being evasive*, she thought, *as if he still doesn't completely trust me.*

"Did you hide anything else?" she ventured quietly.

He thought about that. "I didn't, but some workmen hid some tools they were using. They were in a box."

"Tools?" she asked weakly, thinking of the diamonds, "do you remember where they were?" She held her breath.

"Cutting instruments." He thought a moment. "I believe they were in that tunnel somewhere." He pointed to the opening where Yuri had gone. "It's blocked now."

"There's something I don't understand," she asked. "If you hid the tablets near here, and no one else has touched them, and that's where I found them, then we're close to where I was digging. Where are we? What is this place?"

"We're underneath the great city called Montoba. It runs several hundred kilometers from end to end. It's been destroyed by the wars and the fiery mountain."

"Destroyed? How? What do you mean 'wars'?"

"The tribe from the lower ground, the Dungé we call them, tried to conquer the world. The other tribes, the Midé and the Élevé, banded together to save themselves."

"Who won?"

"What?"

"The war! Who won the war?"

"No one really wins wars. Almost everyone was killed."

"I'm sorry. I'm confused. Which tribe are you from?"

"The Midé. There're not many of us left."

17

"Your allies, the Elévé? Are there many of them left?"

"No. But the most important one may be. Their leader."

"Who's that?"

"The Princess. She's missing."

"What happened to her?"

"We don't know. She disappeared many years ago."

Archie felt she wasn't being told everything.

"Who is that statue at the head of the entrance with rocks in front?"

"That's the Great King, father of the Princess."

Archie thought a moment. "You talked about the mountain? What about **it**?"

"It's not a mountain anymore, but we still call it the mountain. Legend says the mountain blew up long ago and became a huge, long, deep lake. Everyone's afraid of it. A cloud comes from the lake and kills everyone nearby."

"A cloud?" Archie thought about this for a moment. This sounded vaguely familiar to something she'd read about.

"How do they die?" she continued, "from suffocation?"

"No one knows. The cloud comes from nowhere and just rolls across the land, killing everything for miles around."

"I think I know what it is. It's carbon 13!"

"What's that?" asked the leprechaun, staring with awe.

"It comes from underground, deep below the bottom of the lake. It accumulates over a period of many years. And then something happens, like an earthquake or landslide, and releases it. It then rises and generates a thick cloud of carbon dioxide. We've had some killer lakes that…"

Archie was interrupted by another rumbling noise and the ground shook again. *It was a bit stronger but still no need to worry,* she thought. But that was all Pre needed.

"Let's go. It's not safe and it's a long journey."

Archie was more worried about the urgency in Pre's voice than the shaking. *He'd waited a long time. Why the urgency now?* she thought. She persisted in her questioning.

"Yuri'll be back soon. Did you write the tablets?"

"Some of them," he mumbled. "Where is he? We must go. We don't have much time."

"Why are you so worried? Much time for what?"

He hesitated. "It's the mountain. It's getting worse." They heard sounds coming from the cave Yuri had entered and they turned.

"I hear Yuri. He'll be here soon. Do you know what these drawings on the wall mean? Did you carve them?"

"Some of them." Pre was looking at each passageway and acting now as if someone or something would come at any moment, like one of those terrifying creatures he'd mentioned. "They tell about the wars we fought," Pre said in a low voice, "and the terrible mountain."

"What's this?" Archie pointed at a strange drawing on the wall. There were six appendages: two in the front which looked like two legs; two others in the back which looked like wings; and two others which were like arms pointing upward. All were attached to a carapace or shell which gave the appearance of a beetle, as did the beady little eyes. "It's a beetle with arms!" she burst out.

Before Pre could answer, Yuri burst from the cave, holding a small creature. It looked like a dwarf to Archie. Yuri was holding an axe, and the creature was dragging a large sack. It was short and stocky, wearing rumpled dusty gray clothes. It had a loose pointed hat or cap. It looked frightened, and pulled back when it saw them.

"Look what I found," Yuri yelled, "some sort of dwarf."

"He's a gnome." Pre responded quickly, and talked to the gnome in a different language. "Reaye ouye koye?"

"Ye asweye raidafye utbeye eheye iddeye otneye urtheye emeye."

"Troduceinye ourelfseye!" answered Pre.

Yuri wished they'd stop talking in this strange tongue.

"Oh, hello. My name's Murgi," said the gnome.

"He's a friend," explained Pre. "He wants to go with us." Yuri decided to return the axe to the gnome.

"What's in your sack?" Yuri leaned forward, peering into the sack. "Can we look?"

"Presents," answered Murgi, as he reached into the sack. "We've been waiting for you." He pulled out two rapiers. "These are for you. You'll need them on our quest." Pre took one from Murgi and held it in his hand.

"They're very sharp. They have diamond points. Here!" Pre handed the rapier to Yuri. He turned to Archie. "They're made from the same material as the tablet sheets you found. Very light and strong."

Murgi looked at Archie. He spoke to her hesitantly.

"Are you...are you...a female? A woman? Our women were all warriors, but I didn't think that your women were." Archie interrupted him and laughed.

"Oh, don't worry." Archie pulled a pin from her hair and let her hair fall down her shoulders and back. *Perhaps that's enough to show him I'm a woman*, she thought. She took the rapier from Murgi. "Our women were not involved in fighting for two hundred years, but years ago we became warriors, as you would say. I can fight as well as any man." Archie brandished her sword and Murgi jumped back.

Pre held up his hand and Archie put her sword down. Pre reached into Murgi's sack, and pulled out several orange wafers. He turned to Archie.

"Did you bring those other wafers?"

Archie pulled out the two gray wafers she had saved.

"Yes, why?" she asked curiously. Pre smiled.

"Good! You'll need them some day." He handed Archie and Yuri two orange wafers each. "Don't get these mixed up. We wouldn't want to lose you. These orange ones are to eat, for food. One will last you a very long time. This is one of our secret inventions."

Archie put all her wafers into her backpack. Yuri did the same. Pre then pulled an instrument from the sack that looked like a recorder to Yuri. Pre smiled then put it back. He was satisfied.

Yuri turned to Murgi. "How'd you know we're going on a journey?"

Murgi looked at Pre to see if it was okay to say anything. Pre nodded.

"I want to go with you. We must save our lady!" Murgi blurted out. "I want to get back at..." Pre held up his hand to stop the gnome from saying any more. "Well, what I mean is, you'll need a strong arm."

There was a noise coming from the Boulder passageway.

Pre yelled, "Hurry. There's no time to tell you anymore." Pre ran into the King tunnel, away from the noise. Archie dashed after him, Yuri grabbed his backpack and the sack and chased after them, then Murgi grabbed his axe and followed.

After they had disappeared, the noise from the passageway grew louder, and a tall, dark, imposing, hooded figure, dressed all in black, swooped into the cavern. His hood shadowed his eyes, so that they seemed the merest black speck as he peered out. He stopped and listened for any sounds.

A short, ugly, misshapen goblin followed closely behind him. He was dressed in saggy, dirty, gray clothes, and also had a hooded cape over his head. Each figure carried a staff which he used as a walking stick: the tall figure held a very long one as high as his head, and the short figure a very small one barely up to his waist. The tall figure spoke first.

"Iddaz onyaz earhaz hattaz oisenaz? Eeplpaz?"

"Yaz. Everalsaz oicevaz."

"Igor!" the tall figure spoke harshly. "I heard voices." He listened and looked at each of the other entrances, but there was no sound.

"Yes, Master Scarth. So did I," answered Igor.

"Don't use my name, you miserable ugly dwarf." Scarth snapped at Igor.

"Yes, master. As you say." Igor feigned subservience.

"I **did** say. Let's get on with it. After them, you slimy toad." Scarth moved to the King passageway. Igor followed with quick small steps, trying to keep up with his tall master.

"Why are we following them?" Igor whined.

"They'll lead us to the princess. Don't ask questions. Let's go!" Scarth strode swiftly out of the cavern.

As the footsteps of Scarth and Igor faded slowly in the tunnel, a light airy fairy tiptoed out from the Pebble passageway. Her diaphanous wings fluttered, and her shimmering gossamer dress seemed to be made of cobwebs. She wore small dainty pointed shoes.

She listened, then let out a terrifying noise, like a scream, then used her wand to direct the noise into the Pebble passageway. She did this periodically, as if the noise were fading. She then hid in the cave.

Scarth and Igor rushed in, and heard the fading noises.

"They tricked us. They must have been hiding in the cave, then ran into this other passageway. Quickly!" Scarth rushed past the pebbles marking the entrance toward the noises.

"Yes, master, as you wish. Stupid idiot." Igor made a face and mimicked Scarth, then raised his arm and clenched his fist and arm in a disrespectful sign.

"Hurry!" yelled Scarth from the tunnel.

"Yes, master. As you wish. Coming." Igor shuffled off.

The fairy darted out from the cave she was hiding in, and flew after Pre and the group through the King tunnel, away from the evil Scarth. She had done her job well. They would have a little more time to escape!

Diaphanous wings

Shimmering gossamer dress

Dainty pointed shoes.

FOUR

The Days of the Great King

Princess Mia woke once again to the sound of the stream. Other than the tiny trickle, the dark oppressive silence was all too familiar. She'd been captive in this dungeon, or tomb as she thought of it, for so long she could no longer count the days. Food wafers had run out some weeks before, and she was very weak. Only the water and long bouts of sleep, as if hibernating, had kept her alive. As usual, her memories comforted her.

Princess Mia's earliest recollections were those of being a small child sitting on the knee of her grandfather, the King. She listened to his stories of the early days of the war, a terrible conflict over control of land and resources. The dark forces from the underground, the Dungé, started the war and soon had the Elévé on their heels, in full retreat. The Elévé, the rulers, lived on the highest parts of the city. They were able to stop the advances only after forming an alliance with the Midé, who lived around the rim of the great lake, between the two tribes. Her grandfather told her of the great battles he led, the victories in particular. She never tired of hearing these stories of danger and valor.

He told her how they fought battles above ground and all around the lake, and how the battles spread to the outlying settlements way beyond the rim of the mountain. Eventually, after the Midé joined the war, the Dungé retreated below ground, and the war continued deep into the vast labyrinth of passageways below the high places. The Dungé finally surrendered after many lives were lost.

A long period of prosperity and peace followed the war, and the building of the great city continued at a furious pace. It was magnificent, she remembered, with high towers and walkways high in the sky. Her grandfather retired as King, and her father became the new leader. She often walked with him, gazing with awe as the vast city took shape around her. The buildings and parapets and arches and gardens and bridges continued as far as her eye could see.

She learned that the high towers were part of the vast energy system above and below ground. They collected sunlight and directed the energy down to the surface. Below ground the tunnels had special geothermal energy collection devices that went close to the vast heated underground magma chamber. This was converted to energy and directed back to a central site as well. All this energy allowed the city to be filled with twinkling beacons at night.

She loved these long walks with her father, and used these precious moments to ask questions of him about everything she saw and heard. She learned valuable lessons about architecture and building, energy, and the many inventions of this society. It was during this period that her father started writing his journal on the tablets. They would discuss aspects of it and she sometimes would offer comments.

"Ummm!" he would mumble, "I'll have to say something about that."

But always she would look forward to the stories from her grandfather before she went to sleep. As she grew older, the nature of the stories changed. She had always asked many questions, much to the amusement of her grandfather, but as she grew more knowledgeable, she wanted to know more about their ancient history and their ancestors.

One of the topics she learned to avoid was the subject of her mother, who had died shortly after she was born. When she asked about her, neither Mia's father nor grandfather wished to discuss it. What she learned, she learned from other close members of the family. She learned that her mother was considered the most beautiful woman in the land. She had many suitors but fell in love with her father. It was a storybook romance, and Mia was the only child. But when she asked how she died, everyone changed the subject. So she learned to ask questions about the past that were less personal, and much more general.

What had happened in the distant past to create this land? Why had they decided to live here? How long had their people lived here? Where did they come from? How did the wild dangerous creatures get here? As she peppered questions at her grandfather, he would laugh at her endless energy, persistence, and curiosity. He would explain as best as he could, from the legends that had been passed down. But she was never completely satisfied with the answers. Sometimes during a long session, he would pause.

"Don't stop, Grandfather. Tell me more," she would plead, and he would go on.

"It's time for bed, little one," he would finally say, "we'll continue tomorrow." He would always say this very gently, and she knew he would continue the next day. That is, until one day when she was twelve years old, her father came to her to tell her of the passing of her grandfather. From that day, many things changed.

She seemed to grow up over night. She felt that she had matured rapidly, not just physically, but emotionally. The way she looked at the young Prince Peter of the Midé was different now. He was two years older and that made a big difference when they were young children, but now as she approached her teens, that difference disappeared. At first she became a little shy, then as her confidence in her emerging womanhood grew, she was more at ease with him. He became the one ill at ease. She teased him relentlessly, she knew. She was sure he liked her but was afraid to say so.

Nevertheless, their friendship and romance grew steadily. They spent more and more time together. They talked about every imaginable subject from scientific subjects to more personal ones involving how they felt, and what was important, and what they wanted to do. She was delighted he shared her curiosity, her desire to learn, to explore topics, to discuss everything. They talked endlessly. In their discussions, no subject escaped their scrutiny, including frank discussions about their parents.

During this same period, her talks with her father became much more serious and grown up. They talked almost as equals. He made her realize that one day she would become the leader of the Elévé and of this great magnificent city. He felt an urgency to make sure she understood not only about what leadership meant, but also about the many inventions and the intricacies of the energy systems. They spent hours together talking and talking. Often after they finished talking, he would spend time writing in the journal.

When her grandfather died, her father, who was known as the Great King, had already become fully responsible for the kingdom. It was at the zenith of its power and glory. But sinister forces were at work. Shortly after the death of the old king, during the period of mourning, the Dungé saw their opportunity. Thinking the new king was young and inexperienced, and preoccupied with his father's death and matters of state, they struck without warning. This first time he was able to repel this sudden attack, but he was clearly shaken, and vowed never to be surprised again.

From that time on, the mood of her father changed. He worked furiously on the journal. One day he disappeared on a long journey and did not return for weeks. When he finally did return he spent even more time in the journal writing, thinking and writing.

But the Dungé did not give up. They regrouped, built up their army secretly below ground, and one year later, launched an all out assault that could not be stopped. The princess and her father retreated to a safer haven far from the center of action.

During the first month of the war, the first of a series of terrible events occurred. Prince Peter's father, the leader of the Midé, was killed in the fighting. Worse than that, at least to the Princess, Prince Peter disappeared. The Midé were leaderless and floundered.

The Great King took complete command of the combined army, and spent all of his time at the front. He had entrusted the journal to her keeping, but she did not have the heart to write in it. She was alone at first, but soon she was joined by a companion, a leprechaun from the Midé, that her father had encountered and had sent to her. The leprechaun soon became her confidant and friend.

The Great King and his dwindling troops fought the Dungé fiercely, above ground at the highest elevations, and below ground in the deepest tunnels. The Dungé too were losing most of their fighting forces. In fact, the entire population was slowly being decimated by the war and the military inventions by both sides. The civilian population on both sides was so integrated into the military that they too died in great numbers.

During this dangerous period, the Princess stayed away from the action. She developed a close friendship with her companion, the quiet and taciturn leprechaun. She was quite surprised how rapidly they became friends and how much they seemed to enjoy each other's company. She did not have the heart to write in her father's journal, but the leprechaun took up this duty as a favor to the Great King, and to the Princess.

The fighting continued relentlessly for nearly two years until there were few people left to fight. Finally a truce was declared since there was no winner and the few remaining survivors did not have the heart or means to continue. Many continued to die of wounds received during the fighting, and then starvation steadily took many of the remaining.

And then at the lowest point, another tragedy occurred, the worst yet in the life of the young princess. Her father, the Great King, mysteriously died. Some claimed he was poisoned. The princess was thrust suddenly into the center of affairs. She was now the leader of the small remaining band of Elévé, and by default, the Midé as well.

The Dungé took advantage of this situation and decided to launch another attack, albeit a feeble one. The princess and her small forces managed to repel this with a struggle, but she and the leprechaun, her staunch general as it were, realized that things were very precarious. They had to do something dramatic to save what was left of mankind.

They decided the leprechaun would stay behind while the princess went on a long journey to find the location of the treasure trove she knew her father had created some years before. He had created this for just such a purpose. In his prescience, and with a sense of foreboding, he saw the possibility that the planet might come to just such a state. As he was dying in her arms, her father divulged the contents of the treasure to the princess. She in turn had told her trusted companion. Only the two of them knew how important the treasure was to their survival and to what was left of mankind.

She would be embarking on a perilous journey, they both knew, but she had to do it. They realized they were on the brink of extinction. The city had been destroyed, people were still dying of starvation, and the continuing struggle to control the kingdom was not resolved. A resumption of war would push them closer to the brink.

Things were very quiet for the moment. The few remaining people had disappeared into different parts of the vast city, searching for food of some

25

sort, struggling to stay alive. As if that were not enough, the ominous rumblings from underground added to the tension and fear that all felt.

The princess said goodbye to her only companion, knowing they might not see each other again. She carried only a few clothes in a small backpack. In a small fanny pack she also carried food wafers, enough for a long journey. She hoped to return within weeks, but the many dangers she might encounter might extend the date of her return. The leprechaun retreated to a hidden place below ground and awaited her return. The princess traveled underground, sometimes on the surface at night, but always carefully, always on the alert. She found it very difficult to find time to sleep, dozing only for brief moments, knowing she must be on the lookout. This lack of sleep slowly took its toll and she became less and less alert to danger. She knew she was entering a dangerous state but knew she had to press on and could not chance falling asleep without a guard.

She had been traveling for weeks, slowly but steadily moving toward her target, and knew she was getting closer. She only knew the general location where her father had hidden the treasure as he had died before he could explain in detail. If only she could find the secret site quickly before she dropped from exhaustion.

As she worked her way through the maze of passages, she suddenly sensed she was being followed. She thought she'd heard footsteps. She would stop but then the noises would stop, so she would continue. This went on for some hours and then it happened. The last thing she remembered was the sudden rush of feet. She started to turn toward her attacker, saw the emblem of the Dungé on his sleeve, but was not able to see his face before she was hit on the head.

Vast splendid city.

Memories: destruction, death.

Weak, starving, cave-trapped.

FIVE

The Two WOOs and the Mirror

The band of four, Pre the leprechaun, Yuri and Archie, and Murgi the gnome, were unaware they were being followed. They traveled for many hours and came to another chamber in the vast underground labyrinth of passageways. It was smaller but similar to the first one. Archie observed that the passages continued on and on but always seemed to have a cavern or clearing on a regular basis.

This cavern had a much lower ceiling than the first and quite a bit of rubble was scattered around, including very large boulders. A large amount of moss was growing on the walls, perhaps from a nearby underwater spring. The cavern had a slight musty smell and was stuffy and warmer but still seemed to have a fresh air source from somewhere. She wondered how air could get down into these passageways. Perhaps, she mused, some went up to the surface.

Besides the moss covered entrance through which they'd entered the cavern, there didn't appear to be a passageway allowing them to continue. This didn't bother Pre as he sat on a rock, wiping his forehead with his tattered green sleeve.

"Whew, that was a long stretch. I need a rest," Pre mumbled.

Unlike the other cavern there was no worn path showing the direction generally traveled. *This must not be a well traveled route*, thought Archie. Chair sized rocks were left all around the clearing as places to rest on. She laughed to herself when she thought of this as the crude furniture of the chamber. They seemed to be equally spaced all around the perimeter.

Yuri wasted no time in checking out his surroundings. He looked around, and spied the entrance to a cave partially hidden by dangling moss and rocks. It had no visible tracks going to it, so he surmised it was a little used cave.

"Look! A cave," he pointed, "there's no sign of anyone. I'll check it out while you rest," he uttered as he moved rapidly toward the entrance.

"Be careful, Yuri!" Archie urged. "Pre told me about the dangerous creatures that roam around here."

"I'll go with him, my lady." Murgi hoisted his axe over his shoulder and followed Yuri toward the cave entrance.

"Don't take too long," Pre counseled. "We must keep moving. It wouldn't surprise me if we're being followed."

"We'll be right back." Yuri drew his sword, made a mock thrust, growled and bared his teeth. He yelled theatrically, "Whatever you are, prepare to die!" Yuri and Murgi charged into the cave.

"Oh, Yuri," Archie muttered, "you are such a kid."

"Pre," she turned to him, "back there, before we dashed out of that cavern, Murgi said something about saving our lady? Is that the princess?"

"Yes. We think she's in danger. If she's still alive."

"Is that where we're going to find the treasure?"

"She was trying to find the treasure site. We know the general area where it's hidden. I'm hoping we find her somewhere near there."

"You said you thought we're being followed," she pressed on, "by whom?"

"We don't know," Pre shrugged. "Perhaps our enemies. We can't take any chances."

"We've been traveling for hours," she blurted impatiently, "up and down hill, through twists and turns. It keeps getting hotter and hotter, then cool again as we climb back up. Why? Where are we?"

"These passages go several kilometers below ground." He was more patient and took time to explain. "The deeper we go, the closer we get to the tunnels that go in close to the magma chamber. We get heat and energy from it."

"Now I understand!" She became calmer. Now was a good time to ask her other questions. "No matter how deep we go, the passageways always seem to have some light. Why is that? Where's the light come from?"

"Phosphorescence."

"What?"

"It's hard to explain. The persistent emission of light from rock formations. They have lots of phosphorescence."

"The air is always fresh. How does it get down here?"

"Usually just through the tunnels but in some places they drilled vents you can't see."

"I understand." She pointed to a small opening away from where they entered. "Is that the way we go?"

Pre laughed. "No, that's another cave. The main passageway is hidden. Remember the riddle in the journal? About the eggs?"

"Yes. That was easy. A lady sells half the eggs and half an egg more three times and then the eggs are gone. But what does that have to do with this?"

"The journal mentioned the rock chairs?"

"Oh, I get it! Count the chairs. The number of eggs." Archie walked along counting the rock chairs. "Alright, I'm here. Now what?"

"Give it a push." Pre chortled.

She did and to Archie's amazement a boulder behind the chair moved and opened an entrance to a small passageway.

"It'll close behind us when we leave here."

"Why the hidden tunnel and the riddle?"

"For anyone following, it would stop them if they don't know the riddle and the answer."

Archie was silent for a moment. "How much farther do we have to go?"

"I'm sorry, my lady," Pre answered, "but this is a long journey. We still have the dangerous part ahead."

"Why? What do you mean? What's ahead?"

"We have the lake to cross." Before Pre could continue, Yuri and Murgi backed out of the moss covered cave entrance, with sword drawn and axe raised. They were followed by two creatures, one tall and one short, who were holding black wands in their hands. The short one also had a staff in its hand but did not appear to know how to use it.

"What are those things?" Archie turned to Pre.

"Elves," answered Pre. "I know they don't look like normal elves."

There was nothing elegant or majestic about these pathetic looking elves. They were dressed in drab, shabby, and dirty rags that had once been elegant black form-fitting outfits. Their faces were covered with dirt and grime. They advanced on Yuri and Murgi.

"You'll taste my sword. Prepare to die!" Yuri yelled.

"Yuri!" Archie interjected. "They look so pathetic. Don't hurt them."

"Shall we turn them to stones?" asked the tall elf.

"No, let's turn them to bones," answered the short one.

"Reduce them to dust?"

"We'll do what we must."

"Let's turn them into fools."

"Or, better yet, to mules."

The two elves looked at each other and spoke in unison.

"They'll never tell
We cast a spell!"

They raised their wands together as if they were about to cast a spell over the group. The staff hung loosely in the hand of the short elf. Before they could cast the spell, Pre stepped forward and raised his staff.

"Alaca wheez, doodela freeze," he chanted. The two elves froze with their wands suspended in the air.

"Wow! That was close." Yuri, who had been stepping backward, came forward to look at them. "What **are** they?"

"They're called the TWO WOOs, WOOWON and WOOTU," Pre answered. "They're probably the only elves that survived the wars. They're a bit mischievous, but generally harmless. Let's not take a chance though. Take their wands. And that staff," he yelled. Yuri stepped forward, took the wands from their upraised hands, and Murgi took the staff. Pre continued, "Alaca wheez, undothe freeze!" The WOOs relaxed and returned to normal. They looked chagrined.

"They seem so forlorn and woebegone," Archie sighed, "could they really cast a spell? They seem so pathetic."

29

"They certainly could. Especially with that staff, **if** they knew how to use it," Pre said to Yuri. "Yuri, hold on to it!"

"The staff?" Yuri stepped toward Murgi, who held it up. "What's so dangerous about the staff?"

"It's a **wizard's** staff!" Pre spoke emphatically.

Murgi gave the staff to Yuri, who put it in the sack. "What are you elves up to?" Murgi muttered under his breath as he drifted back in the direction of the cave. Pre turned and resumed speaking to the elves. "Now, behave yourself. Your oath?" Murgi disappeared into the cave.

"We won't harm anyone.

We're just having some fun," chanted the elves.

"On your oath. Promise!" Pre insisted. The two WOOs reluctantly agreed. "OK! OK!

We will, we say

Though we are really loath

To promise on our oath.

May we sleep and never wake

If we our promise break!"

Pre nodded to Yuri. Yuri gave the WOOs back their wands. During this exchange, Murgi had searched the cave. He came out with a small oval mirror in his hand.

"What's that?" Archie asked.

"It's our missing mirror!" Pre jumped in and turned to the two WOOs. "You stole it!"

"We didn't, we swear.

We found it in there.

In these very dark places,

We love to see our faces."

The two WOOs moved over to the mirror and preened in front of it.

"Found it with the staff?" Pre said to the WOOs and they nodded yes. Pre turned to Archie. "I believe them. This was lost long ago. It's a magic mirror. But, alas, the password was also lost, with the Great King."

"The Great King?" she asked.

"He was killed in the war." Archie was looking quizzically at Pre. He nodded his head. "Yes, **he** was the one who started writing the tablets." Yuri and Murgi had moved over and were looking curiously at the mirror.

"Abracadabra!" tried Yuri. He waved his hands in front of the mirror. Nothing happened.

"Ackle dackle doodle!" Murgi tried his luck.

"No. No. Let me think," interceded Archie. She thought for a moment, then looked in her notes. "Yes, there was a mention of a mirror. And, Penaw, Penay...Let's see – I think it went: 'Penoyourecretse'".

There was a puff of smoke and the princess appeared in the mirror. She was sitting on a cave floor and looked very tired. She spoke in a clear, but weak, subdued voice.

"Oh, help me. Come quickly. I fear I'll die soon."

"Princess, can you hear me?" Pre spoke with a sense of fear in his voice.

"Oh, Pre! It's you. I ran out of food wafers – my last one must've been a month or two ago. I'm getting weaker and weaker. The only thing I've had in all that time is water from a small stream running through here."

"My lady, I couldn't get to you sooner but now I have some help. Where are you?"

"In a cave near the Beetle. I almost made it but they caught me and locked me in here."

"Who, my lady?" interjected Murgi.

"I don't know. I was knocked out and came to in this cave. Please help me."

"We will, Princess. We will. We're coming!"

"Please come soon. I can't last much longer."

"Just wait until we find who did this to you, Princess! I'll take my axe and…"

"Pre, I couldn't solve the last riddle," said the princess.

Archie interjected. "Which one? About the coconuts?"

"I solved that one. No, I mean the other one. I don't know what I'll do now!" The image of the princess in the mirror slowly faded away.

"There's no time to waste," Pre urged. "We must hurry."

There was a loud noise from the moss covered tunnel. They all prepared for an attack, with swords, axe, wands, and staffs raised and ready. The fairy rushed in, out of breath, looking at the passageway from which they all had emerged.

"Wow! I finally caught up with you. You were moving so quickly."

"Who are you?" Yuri spoke firmly with his sword raised.

"She's a good fairy. Her name is Calypso." Pre interceded as he pushed Yuri's sword down. "What is it, Calypso? You look worried."

"You're being followed!" Calypso was still out of breath. "Scarth and Igor are tracking you. I tricked them but they won't fall for that again. You'd better leave here."

"Scarth?" Archie asked. "Who's he? Why's he following us?"

"The evil leader of the Dungé," said Calypso. "He's after the Princess."

"I'm confused," Archie persisted. "If he's following us, then he doesn't know where she is, but he thinks we do?"

"I think I can explain," Pre stepped in. "Some time ago, we intercepted a bandit that was on his way to the Dungé, to collect a reward in exchange for information about the location of the Princess. Then he tried to bargain with us."

"Asking a ransom, you mean?" asked Yuri.

"You could call it that," Pre agreed. "We refused. He tried to escape, and in the fight, he killed himself, before we could find out where he had locked up the princess."

"So Scarth found out about the bandit?" Archie queried.

"We're pretty sure Scarth hired him," Pre answered, "and furthermore, we believe this bandit was the one responsible for the death of Mia's mother."

"Her mother?" Archie was stunned and confused.

"Mia doesn't know this. Shortly after she was born, her mother was attacked by two bandits who tried to capture her for ransom. Her mother fought like a tigress and killed one of the bandits but the other one stabbed her in the back. The entire kingdom mourned her death."

"How terrible. Poor Mia!" As she was speaking, the rumbling and shaking of the ground began again, this time even stronger than before.

"Let's go," yelled Pre. He headed toward the secret hidden tunnel and the others followed. As they were leaving several rocks fell from the ceiling of the cavern onto the floor. "Maybe these falling rocks will slow them down. Let's get far from here." Pre ran into the passageway followed by Archie, Calypso, the two WOOs, Yuri, and Murgi. The rock covering the hidden tunnel closed behind them. The small group of four had now grown to a stalwart, united band of seven, with a common purpose: to save the Princess!

Phosphorescence. Elves.

Magic mirror, vision, fear.

Rumbling. Shaking. Rocks.

SIX

Screaming Meemies and Tenty

The hardy, resolute band of companions now marched with a greater sense of unity and urgency after the visitation from Princess Mia. Murgi, in particular, marched with a furious pace to save "his lady"! With the addition of the TWOWOOs and Calypso, the team was formidable. After marching for two days, they entered another large cavern.

Archie emerged through a sparkling, crystal archway, followed by Yuri, Murgi, Pre, Calypso, and the WOOs. Archie was stunned by the beauty of the chamber. All the walls were crystal, glittering in the light. *Could they contain diamonds?* Archie wondered. The archway added to the beauty of the cavern. From the archway there were two paths leading to two other passageways. One was larger than the other and had a square crystal rim at the entrance. Archie thought this passage entry point was lovely but not as beautiful as the archway. The other entrance was smaller and plain without any crystal around it, but it did have some moss growing around the rim. She called the passageways Archie after herself, Square, and Moss. A small cave was carved from the crystal walls and the fallen debris was placed at the entrance.

Murgi had his axe, Pre his staff, Calypso and the WOOs their wands. Archie and Yuri each had a sword and backpack and Yuri also dragged Murgi's sack. *We are well armed,* mused Archie.

Archie perceived that the air was slightly fresher and cooler than in the previous cavern, but the light was still dim. She thought the cool air meant they were getting closer to the surface. She was tired of these long dark underground passages. She'd love to see the light of day.

The annoying and mischievous WOOs teased Murgi, pulling his coat and hair. He tried his best to ignore them.

"Look, it's a fork in the path," Murgi exclaimed, swatting at WOOTU's hand. "Which way do we go, Pre?"

"Let me think a moment," he responded.

The TWOWOOs rhymed alternately

"Which fork will we take?

What choice will we make?

If we take the right turn

Then who knows what we'll learn?

If the right path we take

Then t'will lead to the lake!"

"Quiet!" screamed Pre. "It's been many years since.."

Pre was not able to finish his thought. Terrible shrieking, screaming sounds came from the Square entry. Half a dozen of the most hideous, small, nerve-wracking creatures ever imagined came streaming in. They were ragged in their looks, wearing threadbare, dirty, ratty, shifts that barely covered them. They caught the band of seven by surprise. Their red, wide-eyed look and terrible noises caused the the seven of them to shrink and cower together.

The creatures encircled them, going round and round, trapping everyone in the middle of the clearing, except for Yuri who had drawn back toward Archie, the passageway. He still carried the sack, and drew his sword.

"You'll feel this steel, you wretched creatures."

The surrounded group covered their ears to stop the piercing screams. They dropped to the floor and cowered in the center of the cavern. As the creatures continued to encircle them, the two WOOs tried to use their wands.

"The wands don't work," yelled Pre. "Yuri, the sack."

Yuri waved his sword with one hand to keep the creatures at bay, and reached into the sack with his other.

"Back! You'll taste my sword. Prepare to die." Yuri pulled the recorder from the sack.

"Play it! Play the recorder," Pre screamed above the noise of the shrieking creatures. Yuri played a soft melodic tune that had an immediate effect on the creatures. They slowly sank to the ground.

The other six scrambled to their feet and recovered their composure. They dragged the bodies of the creatures into Archie tunnel. Archie was shaking a bit.

"Wow! That was scary," she spoke quietly. "I didn't know you had such musical talent, Yuri." He gave her a quick look. She turned to Calypso. "What were those?"

"Screaming Meemies. Only soothing sounds work on the Meemies. They attack when you least expect it."

They all stood around quietly until Murgi spoke up.

"Which way do we go now?" He pointed at the two passageways.

"The passage that way," Pre answered and started to move toward Square.

"Pre, the princess mentioned a riddle," Archie stopped him. "Is that the one about a pirate capturing a ship?"

"Yes! How'd you know about the riddle?"

"I found it in the tablets. Yuri and I were puzzled by it."

"Oh! The Great King did that. As well as the other one. I haven't solved either yet."

"Made up riddles?" She was perplexed. "Why?"

"I'm not sure about the coconut riddle but I'll explain about the pirate riddle after we save the princess. Let's keep moving!" Pre moved again to the entrance.

Yuri started to follow Pre but suddenly stopped. "Going through these tunnels is nerve-wracking. Can we go up - travel on the surface?"

"We can," Pre paused, "but we're safer down here."

"Why?" Archie interjected. "What's wrong up there?"

"It's the Flying Furies!" Calypso spoke up. "It's a wasteland. There's no place to hide and the Furies can see for many kilometers. They'd spot us for sure."

"Oh, more hideous creatures? I'm afraid to ask about the Flying Furies, but...What **are** they?"

"They're hard to describe." Pre sought to find the right words. "Hideous! Vicious! They fly like bats, silently, using radar. They have eyes like bugs and sting like bees."

Archie stood in stunned silence. "They sound terrible," was all she could manage to say. Yuri decided to press on.

"Calypso, you said *It's a wasteland.* How'd it get like that?"

"First it was the war," she tried to explain. "Each of the tribes developed such awful weapons. It was terrible. So many were killed. Then the mystery, from the lake. No one knows for sure what it was. Some sort of gas, we think."

"Yuri, remember those killer African lakes?" Archie turned to him and he nodded. "Nyos, Monoon, Kivu? They found that carbon dioxide was trapped at the bottom of these deep lakes. Kivu also had methane in it."

"Yes, I remember," Yuri recalled. "An earthquake or landslide triggered the release of a thick cloud of carbon dioxide. You think that happened here?"

"Much the same," Calypso said. "A cloud came rolling across the land. It killed everything. People. Animals."

"Yes, everything except the Furies," spoke up Pre. "I think they're some kind of mutant. Anyway, they survived and you could say "they rule the skies".

Suddenly there was a thumping from passageway Moss.

"Get ready," yelled Yuri. "Something big is coming."

They drew their swords or raised their staffs or wands and stepped away from the noise. A giant caterpillar slowly squeezed its way through the small opening and came crawling out. It stood as high as Yuri and was three times as long as it was high.

It had fat rolling segments of yellow and green with large black dots. It stood on many legs, each of which was two feet high and half a foot wide. It was an enormous, ugly, bulging creature. Its huge eyes were wide open. It saw them and started to whimper.

"Don't hurt me," it whined. "Please! Don't hurt me." They all turned and looked at each other in amazement.

Murgi stepped forward. "Hurt you? You have to be kidding. A big thing like you? We're afraid you'll kill **us**!"

"Oh, no, I wouldn't hurt a fly. I was afraid you'd make fun of me, just like everyone else does."

35

"We wouldn't do that," said Calypso softly.

"What's your name?" Archie added.

"Tenty! They call me Tenty."

"Tenty, why do they make fun of you?" she went on.

"It's because I'm always eating. I can't stop myself. All I want to do is eat and eat."

"Well, what's wrong with that?"

"I keep getting bigger and bigger. Soon I'll explode."

"I don't think that'll happen. Is that the only problem, Tenty?" Archie spoke gently.

"They call me WMD. The Worm of Mass Destruction. Then they laugh and laugh."

"Oh, don't worry." Archie stepped closer, no longer afraid. "We won't laugh at you."

"Thank you." Tenty was very shy and bashful and the others began to take a liking to this giant gentle creature. They moved forward as Tenty gave a huge yawn. "I've just eaten so much, all I want to do is find a nice quiet place and build a cocoon and curl up and go to sleep. I'm so tired."

Yuri stepped forward and pointed to the small cave entrance. "Just go in that nice quiet place. No one will bother you there." It was clear that it would be a tight fit but he felt Tenty could just get through into it.

"Oh, thank you, thank you." Tenty lumbered over.

"Have a nice sleep," offered Archie.

"I will. And I'll help **you** some day." Tenty squeezed through the cave entrance only by shortening its feet and elongating its body. All the green and yellow bulges and enormous feet disappeared slowly from the sight of the others. Once inside Tenty spun his cocoon web casing around and around from end to end, slowly encasing himself in a protective pupal shell. He then went into a long well deserved metamorphic sleep.

"Well, that's that. Let's get on with this." Pre had started toward passageway Square, but was interrupted.

An enormous roar came from the Archie tunnel. A huge catlike head with two long upper teeth and fierce yellow eyes appeared. The giant beast entered the cavern and roared again. It stood on huge furry legs with giant claws. Its gleaming eyes took in the scene. Another piercing roar shook the cavern.

"What's that?" yelled Archie.

"It's a Saber-Toothed Tiger. Run! It's vicious," screamed Calypso above the roaring.

The band scattered in disarray. The TWOWOOs and Calypso ran into the passageway Moss. In the confusion, Calypso dropped her wand in the middle of the clearing. Pre and Archie ran into the passageway Square. Yuri backed up and waved his sword wildly at the beast.

"Prepare to d...Aaaah!" When the beast continued to move toward him, Yuri ran after Calypso and the WOOs, yelling as he went. As Murgi started to follow after, he saw Calypso's wand and screamed.

"Calypso, you dropped your wand." Realizing it was too late, he grabbed it and ran after Pre and Archie as the tiger was about to catch him. The tiger roared again, then followed Yuri's group.

Scarth had been just behind the tiger and had observed the melee from the safety of the passage behind the archway. He entered shortly after the tiger left, followed by Igor who was sullen and sulking and dragging his heels. Scarth heard a distant roar from the tiger as the beast moved through the Moss passageway.

"I'd rather not tangle with that tiger just now. Maybe he'll do my work for me," he laughed. "Let's follow the other group. Come on, you misshapen sack of scum." He strode through Square after Pre, Archie, and Murgi.

Igor started to follow Scarth. "Yes, Master. As you wish. Whatever you say. You know best." He moved briefly into the passage, but darted back into the clearing. "Master's evil. He calls me names. I'm not following him anymore."

Igor noticed the cave where Tenty had gone. He ran into it.

No sooner had he disappeared than Scarth returned.

"Where'd you go, you wretched reptile, you villainous viper? When I find you, I'll turn you into a toadstool." Scarth spied the small cave and slowly stepped into it. He soon came back into the clearing, shaking himself. "Ugh! A giant slug." He looked around briefly for other possibilities and shrugged. "I'll take care of you later," he muttered and strode quickly after Pre and the others.

Igor slowly slid from the cave, covered all over with bits of the cocoon. He tried in vain to clean it from his clothes, and his skin.

"Aahh, it's sticky. Nasty master. I'll get back at him some day. He'll see," he grumbled and looked back and forth at the two passageways into which the group had scattered. He looked first at the entranceway where Yuri, Calypso and the TWOWOOs had run, followed by the Tiger. He then looked a long time at the larger passageway, where Pre, Archie and Murgi had gone, followed by Scarth.

"Which way will Igor go? Igor will take his chances with the Tiger." He smiled and followed the Tiger and Yuri.

Cocoon encasing
It's the season for change, but
Butterfly or moth?

SEVEN

Shroom Attack

Yuri, Calypso, and the WOOs traveled for many hours to make sure they'd left the vicious tiger behind. The underground passageways meandered up and down. They entered a very large chamber in the maze of tunnels.

Yuri was stunned by the beauty of the chamber. Stalactites hung from the ceiling and were dripping into several warm pools. The stalactites rimmed the chamber.

"Calypso," Yuri asked, "Where do these pools go?"

"They go underwater to thermal pools. They can be hot."

"I wish Archie could see these. They're beautiful."

Yuri realized there was no way out other than the way they entered. There were stalactites around the entrance of the tunnel. There was a moss covered cave, and one wall was smooth with figures engraved. He wondered if there were hidden passages.

The WOOs began tugging on Calypso's wings.

"Quit it. You already made me lose my wand." They decided to retreat, and wait for another time.

Yuri took off his backpack and wiped his brow.

He asked Calypso, "do you notice something strange?"

"Like what?"

"There doesn't seem to be a way to go on. And look at the engravings on the wall." Yuri pointed.

"Looks like a monkey. And those look like coconuts."

"It was mentioned in Archie's journal. It's a riddle."

"What about?" asked Calypso.

"Three men collect some coconuts. Then each in turn divides the pile in thirds with one coconut left over for the monkey. Each hides a third and leaves the other two thirds. At the end they divide the much smaller pile into thirds with one again for the monkey."

"We figure out the number of coconuts? I have it."

"So quickly? You're sure?"

"Yep. Now what?" Calypso asked.

"I guess we walk off the number around the cavern."

Calypso whispered in the ear of each WOO and sent one to the left around the cavern and the other to the right. They walked slowly, counting as they walked. Then each stopped at the same time some distance apart.

"I didn't know which way to go. What now?"

"They should push against the wall as we did before."

Calypso nodded to the WOOs to go ahead. Each tapped the wall with their wands. They jumped back as the rocks slide away in the two spots revealing two passageways. One had moss around the opening, the smaller had an archway. The WOOs named them MOSSIE and ARCHIE as Archie did.

"Well, I'll be," Yuri mumbled. "It's just like the last cavern. I wonder if the passages were supposed to be hidden there but the entrances were left open by mistake? Oh well, it doesn't much matter now."

This cavern was even cooler than the last one and the light was different too. It wasn't just phosphorescence. The light in both of the secret tunnels intensified. *Perhaps they were quite close to the surface*, thought Yuri, *or maybe they were reaching the end of the long series of passageways.*

The TWOWOOs chimed in.

"Which fork do we take?
  What choice do we make?"

"I don't know," Yuri snapped. "Calypso, do you know these tunnels at all?"

"Not very well. Pre would know where they go."

"It looks as if the passageway system is spreading out," stated Yuri, "but is it possible they come back together?"

"I don't know. There are many kilometers of passages in all directions."

"Should we wait? I hope you know because I don't."

"We should go ahead. We've no way of knowing where they are, or whether the others are ahead or behind…."

She was interrupted by violent shaking and rumbling of the ground. The shaking had been occurring periodically, each time seemingly stronger than before, as if they were approaching some sort of epicenter.

"Keep moving," she urged. Yuri began to put on his backpack when there was a loud commotion. Half a dozen misshapen, hideous creatures with distorted bodies, heads, and limbs surged into the clearing from all three tunnels. They were the most gruesome creatures Yuri'd ever seen!

Their bodies were cylindrical stalks topped with wide flat "mushroom" caps. Under the cap each had tiny pinpoint little eyes. They had small wings coming out of the backs of the stalks and little arms emanating from the front. Their withered feet were shaped like roots. These talking, walking, winged, ugly shrooms surrounded them.

The WOOs chanted.

"Oh, what have we here.
They're poison we fear.
Our lives we hold dear.
Oh, death it is near!"

"What are these weird things, Calypso?" Yuri asked.

"They're called Shrooms."

"They're the ugliest misshapen things I've ever seen." Yuri drew his sword and stepped toward them.

"Watch out," she yelled. "They're very dangerous!"

Yuri held out his sword and moved toward them.

"Get back. You'll taste my sword. Prepare to die!" He waved his sword as if to fight with them all at the same time. The shrooms were not impressed with his swordplay and moved closer forming a tight circle around the little party.

"Yuri. Don't!" Calypso yelled. "They're poisonous. If you slash one, its poison will splash all over us. We'll be dead in minutes."

The WOOs whimpered, and cowered in the middle of the clearing.

"If one you dare slash
Its poison will splash.
You'll die in a beat
And turn to raw meat."

The shrooms circled them, chanting and singing.

"Oh my, isn't this sweet? We have something to eat.
Do they taste like raw meat? Or a barrel of wheat?
Do they taste like pig's feet? Or a bog full of peat?
Well, we really don't care, we'll eat all but their hair.
Eat! Eat!
Pig's feet!
Wheat! Peat!
Sweet meat!"

The shrooms closed in around the cowering group.

When all looked lost, a wizard dashed in from the passageway Mossie. He was all white from head to toe. He wore a tall white pointed hat which matched his long white scraggly beard. His white flowing cape reached his pointed white shoes and bloomed out around him. His knobby gnarled hands stuck out from the long wide sleeves.

"It's Sam," shouted Calypso. "You've come just in time."

Sam pulled a wand from his cape. "Alaca balaca calaca freeze!" he intoned.

The shrooms froze in place under Sam's spell. As he recited his incantation, the shrooms slowly dropped to the floor of the cavern, becoming very limp, as if they were melting. They ended up in heaps all about the clearing.

"To the pot we shall take
These slimy shrooms to make
A soup hot and delicious
From these creatures so vicious.
We'll slice them and dice them
Fillet them
Sauté them

40

Add sage and some thyme
A splash of some lime
Then to this thick broth
We'll stir to a froth
We'll have a feast fine
Of sweet shrooms divine!"

"Oh, Sam," Calypso cried. "I thought we were done for. If you'd come a minute later, our journey would be over."

"Oh," Yuri piped in. "I had everything under control."

"Sure, Yuri." Calypso rolled her eyes. "Just as you say."

The WOOs clambered to their feet and chimed in.

"You've come to our rescue
We praise you, we thank you.
Your cape it was flowing.
Your wand it was glowing.
Oh such a wise seer.
You heard our call clear!"

Sam ignored the fawning WOOs. "Here, help me drag the shrooms away. They'll make excellent soup once they're cooked. Fortunately I happen to have a big pot in that cave."

Yuri helped Sam by grabbing a shroom by the wing, which Sam said was not poisonous. Then the others pitched in to drag all the shrooms into the cave.

"I don't see any pot." Calypso peered into the cave.

"Look more closely," Sam countered. With a wave of his wand, a large plain earthen pot appeared next to the pile of shrooms. With another wave of his wand it was filled with boiling water with steam emanating from it and filling the tunnel. "Throw them in and we'll have soup," he ordered. Then he added spices and the soup was ready in no time. Calypso, not to be outdone, borrowed Sam's wand and produced bowls, spoons, and a ladle. With full bowls, they all returned to the clearing to enjoy the soup.

While they were sipping the hot soup, Yuri asked, "What I don't understand, Sam, is where you got all these herbs and spices. You didn't create them with magic, did you?"

Sam smiled, "Why heavens no, Yuri. Hasn't Calypso told you about our special secret Garden? It's just down that passageway a short distance." He pointed to the Archie passageway.

Calypso looked down. "I forgot all about it."

"That's alright Calypso. You've had other things on your mind."

She brightened. "I'll show you when we leave here."

After a brief silence, Sam continued.

"I'm glad my wand worked. I haven't used it in years."

With that, Calypso reached into the sack that Yuri carried, and produced the staff they had found.

"Could that be because you lost something, Sam?"

"My staff! Where'd you find it?" He took the staff.

"Thank the WOOs. They found it. How'd you lose it?"

"I'm too embarrassed to tell you. But having my magic staff will make things easier for what I must do. I'm afraid I can't stay. I have an important mission to do. I'll find you later." Sam moved toward Mossie. The WOOs spoke up together.

"We can both help too.

Can we go with you?"

Yuri and Calypso looked at each other. Then Yuri responded quickly before Sam had a chance to say no. "It's alright with us. Calypso and I will manage without their help." Calypso nodded in agreement.

"Well," said Sam reluctantly, "it was you that found my staff." Sam turned and spoke to the WOOs. "Alright. Come with me. Quickly now." Sam moved swiftly into Mossie and the WOOs followed. WOOTU dashed back in, giggling, and tugged on one of Calypso's wings, before racing back out again.

Calypso sighed deeply. "I'm so glad to get rid of these WOOs. They've been a constant nuisance."

"Well, we'll just have to manage without them," yelled Yuri after the departing Sam. "And their poetry!"

Calypso smiled. "Follow me, Yuri." They left through the Archie passage.

As they left the clearing, the ground shook again violently and the rumbling sounds of an earthquake rippled through the cavern. The echoes bounced off the walls and reverberated throughout the passageways. Rocks fell from the ceiling and onto the floor of the cavern. They'd retreated just in time into the relative safety of the Archie tunnel.

They walked steadily downward. In a few minutes, they entered a huge cavern filled with plants of all kinds and sizes. It was filled with phosphorescenct light, it was quite warm, and moisture dripped from the ceiling.

"Wow!" said Yuri. "This is amazing."

"We found this long ago. The soil is volcanic and very rich. Moisture drips year round from above, and the heat comes from the nearby molten magma chamber. It's perfect for our garden. We have herbs over on the side, tomatoes and corn and beans and squash just about everywhere growing in a tangled mess but we can find them. We even have lots of fruit trees on the side."

"It's huge, and beautiful. And bountiful. Who knows about it?"

"Not very many people besides Pre and Sam and Murgi and I. There aren't very many people left as you know. It's very special and secret. That's why we call it our Secret Garden."

"I wish Archie could be here to see it."

Yuri stared in wonder and began to discover all sorts of vegetables. Calypso touched his arm.

"Yuri! We'd better get going. We have a long trip ahead of us." Yuri nodded and followed Calypso through a small opening that went back up to the Mossie passageway.

Ugly shrooms attack.

By flowing wizard rescued.

Steaming spicy soup.

EIGHT

The Vision of Montoba

Archie was aware of the light increasing as they moved slowly through the passageway. *At last they would be above ground*, she thought. In spite of the danger on the surface, she and Yuri would be glad to get out of the long, poorly lit, and oppressive tunnels. *I hope Yuri's alright*, she reflected. He must have gone the other way, when the Tiger attacked.

Pre was the first to enter the open air from below ground. He stopped after he exited and took a deep breath. He had been moving uphill at a very fast pace to make sure they outran the Tiger. He was followed in rapid order by Archie, and then by Murgi, who was gasping for breath. Murgi was carrying Calypso's wand, and shortly after he entered the open, stuck it securely in his belt. Archie still had her sword and backpack, Murgi his axe, and Pre had his staff. He sat on a rock to recover his breath.

When Archie first emerged from the tunnel she tried to regain her breath and slowly raised her eyes and stared. She gasped. She was stunned at the vastness of the city remains that lay below her and the devastation around her. She tried to get her bearings.

Archie noted there were entryways to the open ground from three places. The party entered from one side of an indentation in the cliff side. There were two other tunnel entrances several meters apart, that went back below ground. One was covered by a thick mass of scraggly vines and the other rimmed by moss. She laughed and called them Scraggly and Old Mossie. The sheer cliff face towered above her on one side. She turned toward the wide open spaces below and viewed the massive ancient city of Montoba lying before her, largely destroyed but still majestic. She wished Yuri could be here with her to see this, when she first glimpsed the city.

It spread far below her in all directions. The landscape where they stood was stark and desolate as far as her eyes could see. There was little vegetation and only a few scraggly trees clinging to life. Otherwise all life appeared to have been destroyed. There were light clouds above them so the lighting was gray – not light and not dark. There were a few rocks scattered around the bare ground amongst the few shrubs and small trees.

"Whew!" Pre was still panting. "I think we're safe now. I haven't heard the tiger following us so it must have chased them. I hope they got away."

"What a steep climb," Murgi gulped. He was still breathing hard. "I haven't done that for a while." He looked around. "Where are we?"

"We're at the highest point on the rim," Pre explained. He pointed way below them. "See the long lake below?"

Archie looked down at the bluish green color of the still water shimmering in the light. She could barely see the opposite shore and could not see either end. The large island in the middle caught her eye. She noticed strange projections around the shore.

"It's huge!" Archie peered all around the edges that she could see in the distance. "What are those things, sticking up?"

"The remains of towers," Pre responded. "They were all along the inside of the rim, overlooking the water. We also had many on the outside of the rim."

"Oh, what a magnificent sight!" exclaimed Archie. In spite of the devastation, Archie had the imagination to envisage the city as it was before it was laid waste by the destruction caused during the wars. She looked up and down and all around, as if to gauge what she was looking at. "Those towers must be half a kilometer high at least."

"You should have seen them before the wars wrecked the city." Pre shook his head with some sadness, yet his voice seemed to have a note of pride in it. "They were twice as high as they are now – they soared more than one kilometer into the sky."

Archie added, "and I can see light glittering on the solar panels – like twinkling stars."

"This city is much bigger than I imagined," Murgi chimed in.

"It's even bigger than what you see from here." Pre waved his arm in a sweeping motion. "You see only the inner city – the part that encircles the lake. The city also encircles the rim on the **outside**. It once stretched several kilometers in all directions." He drew a circle in the air above his head with his arm.

"How did the people get from the outside city to the inside city?" Archie asked with a puzzled expression.

"The passages we've been walking in. That's what they're for." He looked at her with a big smile on his face. "You can cross under the mountain rim through those tunnels. We also used to have gondolas that went up and over the rim. They were very slow but a lovely ride." His voice dropped. "They've all been demolished now." They looked quietly at the sight before them.

"I prefer the tunnels myself." Murgi broke the silence.

"Did you see it before it was destroyed?" Archie turned and looked at him. "It must have been really beautiful."

"I hate to admit it, my lady, but I've never been above ground before," Murgi replied with a subdued voice.

"Never? But you seem to know all about it."

"My grandfather Gormi used to tell us stories about the city – it was our favorite bedtime tale." Murgi brightened up. "We'd say 'Tell us more, Grandpa.' We could never get enough of his stories."

"I never knew either of my grandfathers." Archie spoke in a low voice, barely audible.

Murgi was lost in the past. "He told us about the high towers and the twinkling lights. It was magical. He would describe the space elevators that went high into the sky."

"They had space elevators too? Amazing."

"Yes, my lady, many of them," Pre interjected. "They rose several times higher than the towers."

"Where did they go to?" She looked up and around, trying to imagine them.

"To floating platforms."

"How did they stay in place in the sky?" Murgi asked.

"They were connected and kept in place by a magnetic field," Pre explained but Archie and Murgi continued to look puzzled. "They were very special to us. The whole city was proud of our achievements."

"What were they used for?" Archie pressed on.

"Watch towers," he answered. "If the Dungé tried to attack from outside the city, they could be spotted far in the distance. From that height you could see over the rim surrounding the lake."

"Did they ever attack the city?"

"Many times. We could see many kilometers into the distance on a clear night. They always tried to attack at night and we always saw them and were ready for them."

"I can almost imagine the city as it was before it was ruined," Archie mused. "It must have been lovely."

"It was full of life, teeming with activity." Pre spoke nostalgically. "It was truly a vertical city. There were gardens at many levels. There were courtyards and plazas and beautiful well-kept terraces between the different towers. You could walk all around the city hundreds of feet above ground without ever touching ground level."

"And it went below ground too," Murgi jumped back into the conversation. "My grandfather used to take us on walks around the underground city. The Midé, that was our tribe, actually mingled with the Élevé on the lower city."

"Why didn't you go above?" questioned Archie. "Wouldn't they allow you to?"

"It's not that," Murgi explained. "We could but our people were underground people. We were more comfortable below. We loved the underground nightlife."

"Underground nightlife? What sort of "nightlife"?" she challenged. "I can understand nightlife above ground way up in the air, the plazas and walkways, but what was it like below ground?"

"Well, you know we have those big caverns," Murgi tried his best to describe this world, very special to him. "We had little cafes, and cabarets, and taverns, all around the edges of the caverns. And great beer. Do I ever miss that! Our people would gather in the center and talk and drink."

"Just like they've done for years in the piazzas of Italy and the French plazas," Archie added. "What did you do for light? Wasn't it very dark?"

"Oh, no!" Murgi went on, warming to his subject. "It was sparkling. The elves had given us these magic lights that burned forever, brightly, no matter what conditions we had. We once were great friends with the elves. In some caverns we had great stalactites hanging down, and even stalagmites. The light would bounce off them in all directions. It was magical, it was beautiful." He looked at Archie. "You would have loved the old days, my lady. We had great fun. Lots of singing, and of course, drinking."

"I'm sure I would have loved it, Murgi," she spoke softly, reverently. "Do you think any of those caverns still exist?" She turned to Pre, not sure who would know.

"Well, the caverns perhaps, but not much else." Pre was the first to answer. Then there was a long pause. No one quite knew what to say next.

Finally Archie spoke up. "Pre, what shall we do now? Where shall we go from here? I don't want to go back down there. The tiger might still be lurking below."

Pre pointed toward the vine covered entrance to the passageway Archie called Scraggly. "We should go over there. I think it leads toward the edge of the lake."

Archie did not hesitate and led the way toward the tunnel. "Well, the sooner we get moving the sooner we'll find them," she declared. But just as Archie approached the entrance a large claw lunged out with lightning speed from the darkness of the tunnel and tried to grab her.

"Watch out, Archie," Pre yelled. "Run. It's the flying crab." Pre ran over to Archie and pushed her against the back wall. The giant claw swung wildly and knocked Pre sprawling into the entrance of the other passageway. Archie took a step toward Pre.

"Oh, Pre," she cried out. "Are you hurt?"

The giant claw reached out again and this time grabbed Archie tightly in its claw. Murgi then ran over to try to get Archie out of its grip. He pulled Archie but when that didn't work he battered the claw with his axe, to no avail.

"My lady," he screamed. "I'll get you free." But then the second great claw of the hidden giant creature reached out and grabbed Murgi from behind. Murgi swung his axe ineffectively at the beast before it slipped from his grasp. The large stinger of the crab appeared briefly before the creature disappeared, slowly dragging the two of them into the tunnel.

As Archie disappeared into the tunnel, she yelled out, "Oh, Yuri, help me, help us. I've just been stung. Ohhh!" All was silent. Nothing moved.

Then the flying crab appeared in the clearing. Its huge green body shone in the light. Besides the two large front claws, it had a small pair of legs in the rear of its carapace, shriveled from lack of use, and two enormous wings that had replaced the other small legs. Its stinger projected from its head. Its huge segmented tail dangled down. Its beady eyes darted here and there. It held the two motionless bodies of Archie and Murgi in its giant claws. Then it slowly lifted up and flew into the sky dangling the two of them below it.

Just then Pre dragged himself out of the entrance to the tunnel Old Mossie into which he had been flung. He was groggy. He saw the axe lying on the ground and picked it up.

"What happened?" he mumbled to himself. He looked around. As he recalled what had happened, he looked into the tunnel where he had last seen Archie and the claws of the crab. "The flying crab," he exclaimed, looking up, and slowly his eyes followed the flight of the flying crab as it disappeared in the direction of the lake. He shook his head.

"There's no time to lose," he muttered to himself. "I've got to find Yuri quickly." He shook his head again, then summoned all his strength as he dashed into the vine covered tunnel, which led to the side of the lake where the crossing could be made. This is where he hoped he would find Yuri.

High soaring towers

Twinkling glittering vision.

Cafes. Cabarets.

NINE

The Draken and the Fins

After walking for several hours, Yuri and Calypso emerged from the passageway, and found themselves on the side of a huge body of water. It stretched as far as their eyes could see in all directions, to the left and right, and straight ahead. Far across in the distance, Yuri saw the shore rise sharply to towering cliffs that ringed the lake. It must be very deep, he realized. The soft breeze caused small waves to ripple across the water to the shore he was standing on. It was silent except for the lapping of the water. "So peaceful and lovely," he murmured. "Idyllic, even."

Yuri noticed two small boats on the shore, moored next to them. He also observed another tunnel nearby, almost obscured by brambles, on the edge.

"Calypso, this seems to go on and on. What is it?"

"A huge lake that replaced the mountain thousands of years ago – way before our time."

"What happened to the mountain?"

"It blew up. Water slowly filled in the hole. Now it's surrounded by the remains of the mountain. We've been close to it from the start of our journey."

Yuri looked around and up at the steep cliffs rising rapidly everywhere from the shore. They seemed to go up almost vertically for nearly one kilometer to a ridge that ringed it. He muttered to himself.

"It's a caldera. It must've been a violent mega explosion. I wish Archie were here. This is just like Yellowstone. A giant caldera waiting to explode." He turned back to Calypso. "How big **is** the lake? Do you know?"

"Over a hundred kilometers long, I think," she replied.

"And half again as wide?"

"Almost. But it's narrow here. And there's an island in the middle."

"What do we do now? Do we have to cross it?"

"I'm afraid so. It'd take too long to go around it. I'm pretty sure we cross here. I wish Pre were with us."

"Well, he's not. Maybe he'll find us, but who knows when we'll see Archie and Pre again. Meanwhile we're on our own." He moved toward the two boats on the shoreline. "I'm glad someone left a couple of boats nearby."

"There are boats like these all around. It's a long tradition – they're for anyone to use."

"It's like our tradition back home. When we ran out of oil, people had to start using bicycles. A group got the idea of leaving bicycles everywhere for anyone to use." While he was talking, Yuri beckoned to Calypso to get into one of the boats. She moved toward the nearest one. "Calypso, seeing these boats reminds me of the riddle."

49

"What riddle?"

"The one Archie found in the tablets. Pirates capture a ship and line up all the passengers. The pirate chief will toss overboard some of them at random."

"Oh, but I thought only Pre and the princess knew the riddle. What is it?" Yuri remembered some of its details.

"There are five hundred passengers lined up from bow to stern. The pirate chief puts his mate at the bow and tells the captain he can pick any other spot except the first one. The pirate chief has the numbers two to seven in a tankard and says he'll pick one of the numbers at random. If it's a two he'll throw overboard every other one and stop. The rest will live. The higher the number, the more times he goes through the line to toss people over."

"I don't understand. What if the pirate picks three?"

"He throws over every third person and then goes back and throws over every second one of those still left in line."

"Alright, I think I understand. What if the captain stands in thirteenth place in line? Is he safe?" Calypso climbed into the boat as she spoke.

"He's alright if the number is two or three, or even four, but five will get him. So he's not really safe there." Yuri thought for a moment and exclaimed, "I think I've solved it."

"But no one's been able to solve it!" She helped Yuri step into the boat as he explained.

"I have. The captain has to take the correct number of paces from the bow of the ship to be safe in line. That's the clue to finding the treasure, but we need to find the start, like the bow of the ship." He got in the boat. "I have an idea it's where this beetle thing is. We'd better get going."

Yuri was about to ship the oars and launch the boat when Pre came running in from the passageway with brambles covering the entryway. He was out of breath and looked disheveled. He stood gasping for air trying to get his breath. He still had his staff in his hand and was carrying Murgi's axe. His eyes glazed over.

Pre looked here and there. He appeared disoriented. He could not speak for a moment as he recovered his strength. Pre absentmindedly put the axe in the sack Yuri held.

"Pre," Calypso cried. "What happened? You're alone."

"Where've you been?" Yuri yelled. "Where are Archie and Murgi?"

"They've been kidnapped." Pre cast his eyes down and sank to the ground. He put his hands on his hair.

"Kidnapped?" Calypso responded. "By whom? Scarth?"

"No, the crab."

"Oh, no." Calypso put her hands to her face as she sank onto the seat in the boat.

"What crab?" Yuri stepped out of the boat.

"There's a huge terrible flying crab that hides in the passageways on the edge of the lake." She got out of the boat.

Pre continued, "when we ran up the tunnel to the old city, the crab came out and stung Archie and Murgi."

Yuri put his head down and mumbled to himself softly, "oh, Archie." He turned back to Pre. "What happens when they're stung? Is she hurt? Dead?"

"No, they're just unconscious when the crab stings them. But we have to hurry and find them before it kills them."

Yuri moved to the bramble tunnel. "They're still alive. Let's go." He stopped. "How'd you escape?"

"It knocked me down and I rolled into a tunnel. When I came out, I saw the crab flying in the sky holding them in its claws."

With that Yuri turned and moved back to the boat. "Come on. We need to cross to the other side." But Pre didn't move. Yuri was confused. "Well? What're we waiting for? Let's not waste any more time."

Pre hesitated, "Yuri, the Horned Draken's out there."

"So what, I don't care. We've got to get there before it's too late. Let's move."

So they all climbed into one boat. Calypso climbed in first, picked up a paddle and sat in the bow, Pre in the middle, and Yuri in the stern. He pushed off with a paddle.

To Yuri, these boats had strange shapes, with some characteristics of canoes and others of Viking long boats. They were wide in the middle and tapered in the bow and stern. The stern was high but the bow rose even higher and curved back. The sides were also high and sloped downward into a modest keel. Their draft was deep, he could tell. The three seats were conventional with two crosspieces, but with a high slatted floor to kneel on. The inner construction was of some hard wood, but the outer "skin" was amazing. It was of a synthetic material, quiet as canvas, thinner than aluminum and appeared to be stronger than fiberglass. What was it? He thought of the light metal of the tablets. Perhaps the people of Montoba had invented a flexible thin material for coverings such as this.

The paddling was smooth, fast and effortless in this boat. They started straight across the lake guided somewhat by Pre, who had a general idea where to head. Calypso and Yuri paddled for a couple of hours until they were in the middle. The further from the shore they went, the rougher the water became. They were fighting larger waves. They were getting a little tired and shipped their oars to rest.

With no warning an enormous sea monster rose up out of the water right next to them, and roared. They pulled away in terror. It had huge black eyes and large nostrils blowing fire. Its large wide open mouth was full of jagged sharp teeth. Long curved horns stuck up from the end of its snout. Its purple long tongue loomed over them and flickered in and out. Its eight arms swayed back and forth. It had horny triangular projections along its back from head to tail, connected loosely with webbing. Its skin appeared to be like rough sandpaper.

"What is it?"yelled Yuri.

It breathed fire and roared again. It loomed overhead.

"It's the Horned Draken," yelled Pre. "Get down!"

The dreaded Draken circled the boat, first slowly, then more rapidly, creating waves and the beginning of a whirlpool. The waves became larger. The Draken let out another terrifying loud roar. It waved its eight arms to stir up the water. The boat rocked back and forth.

"We're doomed," screamed Calypso. "Yuri, do something."

The Draken rose up behind the boat, and since it was not able to overturn the boat, attacked with its tentacles. Yuri jumped up, drew his sword, and waved it at the beast.

"Back, you beast. You'll taste my sword. Prepare to die!"

Just at the moment when all seemed lost, a group of sea mammals entered from two directions.

"They're bottle-nosed dolphins," yelled Yuri, "but they have really large heads."

"It's the Fins," yelled Calypso. "Help us."

The Fins swarmed around and around, and began to bump and attack the Draken. They tried to bite the monster but couldn't penetrate the rough hide. They turned their attack to the eight arms and were able to bite off sections of the tentacles. The Draken roared in pain and frustration and tried to get to them with its sharp teeth. The Fins circled around darting in here and there, and increased their attack. The wounded Draken finally disappeared under the water. The Fins all started talking together, excitedly, in rhyme.

"The fighting is done

The battle is won

It has made our day

To chase him away

We can think of times none

When we've had such great fun!"

"You came just in time," exclaimed Calypso. "Thank you. Thank you. I'm sure it would have eaten all of us in a few moments. I **wish** I hadn't lost my wand."

"You saved our lives," chimed in Yuri. "Thank you."

"No thanks needed," spoke up the Head Fin. "We love to attack that big oaf. It gives our lake a bad name."

"Is there anything we can do to repay you?" asked Calypso.

"Well, when you find your wand, you could turn the Draken into a school of fish." He laughed and all the Fins laughed and chattered with him. "Even with a lake as big as this, with all the poison and pollution in it, it's become hard to find enough food."

"I certainly will," agreed Calypso. "As soon as I find my wand." The Head Fin paused and looked serious for a moment.

"What are you doing out on the lake? Where are you trying to get to?"

Pre pointed to the far shore.

"We're trying to find the flying crab before it harms our friends."

"Do you know where it is?" inquired Yuri.

"Of course. Follow us!" The Head Fin started toward the far shore. "We'll give you an escort. That ugly beast won't bother you now."

All the Fins headed off after their leader and the boat followed, with Yuri and Calypso paddling fast trying to ride the wake created by the Fins.

Meanwhile, back on the shore that they'd left some time before, a breathless Igor appeared. He came running in from the tunnel that Yuri and Calypso had come through. He gasped, got his breath back as much as he could, and looked into the distance. "A boat," he mumbled. He quickly clambered into the other boat and paddled slowly after the others.

As Igor reached several hundred meters off shore, Scarth came running in also, but from the bramble tunnel. "Drat! I'm too late," he grumbled.

He saw Igor paddling in the last boat available and shook his fists in the air. "Come back here, you cretin," he screamed loudly, but Igor could barely hear him. "If you don't, I'll find you if it's the last thing I do. I'll find the treasure and kill everyone and kill you too, you swollen bag of dung!" Scarth jumped up and down and hit his fists together.

Igor could see this display from the distant boat. "Master is very angry." Igor spoke to himself. "Igor doesn't think he should go back. Master could hurt Igor if he does. Goodbye, Master," he waved.

"You half-wit, you traitorous slime. When I catch you, I'll turn you into crab bait."

"As you wish, Master. Hee! Hee!" chortled Igor. He disappeared into the distance, as Scarth shook both of his fists at Igor. Finally in frustration Scarth left the shore and went back into the tunnel from which he came.

Tentacles grasping
Thunderous waves spraying water
Surging from the deep.

TEN

Sam and the WOOs

Sam, with the mischievous WOOs in tow, had headed for a distant part of the huge sprawling city, high on a lookout point. He picked this spot where he could survey much of the outer city. Two passageways entering the lookout plateau were distinct. The small one had a rim of scraggly thickets, and the larger one had moss from some source of water. The WOOs called them Scraggly and Mossy. Sam entered first from Mossy, followed slowly by the two WOOs.

The WOOs were breathing heavily, but Sam was not breathing hard at all. "You two are out of shape." They turned away and could not look him in the eye.

Sam looked around in a circle and then faced toward the land below. It had once been green, lush and fertile, with a river slicing through its center. Now the landscape was bleak and ravaged, and the river dried up. A few scattered boulders perched on the bald hillsides. Most of the vegetation had been destroyed except for a very few patches of grass. A few scraggly bushes and tiny trees hanging on to life looked like large distorted scarecrows.

Small groups of people were scattered across the valley, moving slowly. They stood out against the low hills as they herded the few sheep still left, looking for any grazing space or other food they could find. The thin clouds gave the lighting a gray look. The scene had a surreal aspect.

"It looks as if there aren't many people or animals left after all," Sam observed. "I only see a few of them scattered below in Green River Valley."

The WOOs whined in unison.

"We don't see how
  We truly fear
  We can help out now
  Oh learned old seer."

"You certainly can," he turned to WOOWON, "round up those people there." Sam pointed down with one hand. He then turned to WOOTU. "Look for others in the other direction. Then bring them together in the valley. Hurry." With that he pointed with his staff toward the center of the vast Green River Valley.

The WOOs whimpered together.

"What is this here?
  This land of fear?"

"We are in the outer regions of the great city," Sam tried to be patient but he had little sympathy for whining elves. "Stop your whimpering. The people are scared, and don't know what to do. They need leadership. You can help by telling them what to do and where to go."

The WOOs grew quiet and answered simply.

"We'll do what you ask
   Though it's no small task."

"Now, fly!" Sam waved his hand and urged them on. "Come back quickly, and use your wands to speed them up. I'll see if I can find the Head Gryphon." The WOOs went in separate directions to perform their tasks. WOOWON left through Mossy and WOOTU by Scraggly. As they were leaving, Sam whistled very loudly. Soon a large odd creature flew in silently and swiftly from the sky above him. As it settled gently down in front, it slowly folded its wings to its side.

"That was quick indeed, oh Greatest of the Gryphons."

The Gryphon looked somewhat like a flying horse or lion. It was a huge creature with large powerful gray and black wings. Its hind legs and hooves looked like those of a horse, while its front legs and paws, with sharp claws, looked like those of a lion or bird of prey. The head looked like that of a condor with a very big sharp hooked beak.

The hair of the hind legs was smooth and dark and blended in gradually with the thicker tawny hair of the front part. A small mane similar to a lion's encircled its white neck. Its black piercing eyes destroyed the courage of the bravest men.

Fortunately this beast was friendly and loyal. With enemies it could be a fierce fighter, but with Sam it was the most gentle of beasts.

"You called, Master?" The Head Gryphon spoke simply and directly at him. "What can we do to help? I'm sure that's why you beckoned me."

"You're right. You are indeed a wise creature." Sam rewarded it with one of his rare smiles. "Would you round up all the gryphons? For that matter, find any other creatures that can carry people. We need to organize an emergency evacuation of those people remaining here, and we must act quickly. There may be very little time left."

"I'll do as you command," the Gryphon nodded slightly. "May I ask where we will take them?"

"To the Dark Continent."

"The Dark Continent? May I ask why, Master?"

"We will take as many people as your gryphons can carry and start a new civilization there."

"The Dark Continent? Is that not very far away?"

"I'm afraid so. It's several thousand kilometers."

"Many days journey?"

"You are correct. It will take many days flying to get there with them. And.."

Sam suddenly stopped talking. He lowered his eyes.

"And?" the Head Gryphon inquired, waiting.

His voice was barely audible. "I'm afraid you'll not be returning." There, he thought, I've said it. The truth must be known to all.

"I think I understand." The Gryphon nodded his acceptance of this news. "Does it have anything to do with the rumbling of the mountain?"

"You are indeed wise. Thank you for understanding. It is not good news, I know. But make haste. There is no time to lose. You must leave before the day is out. You will lead all the gryphons on this journey and take everyone far from here, as quickly as possible."

"Where shall I assemble all of them as I round them up?"

"In the valley below." Sam pointed to the central area of the huge valley where he had ordered the WOOs to bring all the people they could find. "As we speak, groups of people summoned by the WOOs march toward that central location."

"We'll all be there shortly." The Head Gryphon started to leave and then turned back. "Will there be more that you want done, Master?"

"Yes." He was reminded of his other problem. "I have a special task for you alone. I'll meet you below to explain. It won't take much time. You can help with a difficult situation while the group assembles and begins its long journey. Please extend thanks to your followers for their help. Mankind will owe its continued existence to them."

The Gryphon raised its wings and lifted up into the sky. It flew away effortlessly and silently. Just as it disappeared from one side of the hilltop clearing, WOOWON came dashing in, out of breath and gasping.

WOOWON panted.

"We've completed the task.

 Is there more that you ask?"

"Yes!" Sam ignored the gasping WOO and spoke quickly. "Take WOOTU and wait for the Head Gryphon below until it returns with the other Gryphons. While the group is preparing for a long journey, you'll lead the Head Gryphon quickly back to Yuri and the others. I'll tell you where to meet them."

WOOWON spoke in halting gasping rhymes.

"And why do we need

 This gryphon to lead

 To the group far away

 And again join the fray?"

"There's a special job for the Gryphon to perform." Sam dismissed the WOO. "I'll join you after I check on one last location." Then he snapped his fingers. "One last thing!" He pulled out a magic ball from his pocket. He gave it to WOOWON. "Take this. Give it to Pre. Now, hurry, there's very little time left."

WOOWON did not leave immediately but looked at Sam with a grin.

"And what is this ball?

Perhaps for a wall?"

"You continue to amaze me." Sam shook his head and shrugged. "I don't understand why Yuri and Calypso let you go so easily. You've been such a help."

Then WOOWON left, strutting through the thickets of Scraggly that led down to Green River Valley, while Sam, not bothering with a tunnel at all, flew away far down toward the end of the long valley in search of stragglers.

Fertile Green Valley

Devastated, destroyed.

Dark Continent Bound.

ELEVEN

The Troll and the Flying Crab

In the center of this vast expanse of open water, the waves rose as high as those on the open sea. After many hours of paddling across this rough windy waterway, Yuri's small group saw the outline of the shore. It would have been a lonely forbidding journey for Yuri, Pre, and Calypso without the company of the exuberant fun-loving Fins. They finally reached the far shore.

"Boy, am I glad that's over with," Yuri sighed as they paddled onto shore and beached the boat. They checked out the unfamiliar terrain while the Fins waited offshore.

"Goodbye. Thank you again," the three of them called and waved, as the Fins leaped into the air, somersaulting in unison, and disappeared from sight.

Yuri noticed the beach area was bound at one end with a river that rushed into the lake and a bridge over the river. The river emerged from a passageway one reached at the end of a narrow path. A cave at the other end of the beach was overgrown with vines that partially obscured the opening.

"I'll check out the passage," Yuri announced as he went along the river path and disappeared into the tunnel.

"Let's check out the cave," Pre pointed to the overgrown vine-covered cave entrance. "Calypso, follow me." Pre disappeared into the cave.

"I don't know about this," Calypso muttered, as she cautiously entered. "This could be dangerous."

Yuri returned, dragging a small struggling grotesque creature. It had short fat arms and legs, a roly-poly body, and a bulbous misshapen head. It was not at all happy about being dragged into the sunlight of the open beach.

"Etlay emay elphay onyay!" it muttered.

"What? I can't understand you!"

"Eymay amenay siay ollyray," the Creature stopped briefly, then continued, "oh, sorry, my name is Rolly. Let me help you. I'm a friend."

Calypso returned from the cave. She saw Yuri, but did not immediately see the ugly creature hidden behind him.

"Yuri, Pre went into the cave but I couldn't follow him. It's a pretty big one." Suddenly she spied Rolly. "Who are you?"

"I'm Rolly. I want to help you."

"What are you? What kind of creature are you?"

"Oh, I'm a troll," Rolly answered with a smile. "I thought you knew that. I'm a friend. Can I help?"

"We're looking for a giant crab," Yuri responded. "It flies and…" Rolly held up his hands to show Yuri he didn't need to say anymore, and pointed to the small cave entrance where Pre had gone.

"Say no more. It lives in there. I hate that beast!"

"Lead the way." Yuri waved toward the entrance. "We'll follow."

Rolly held back. "I won't go in. It's very dangerous."

"We **must** go in. I just hope it's not too late." Yuri was determined to go in the cave, no matter what.

Just then Pre came back out, holding his nose. "I found its lair. Smells of crab. Ugh!"

Yuri turned to Rolly, "you said you could help. How?"

"If I get it out in the open, will that help?"

"Yes, I think so," Pre pondered this for a moment. "How will you do that?"

"Wait here." Rolly dashed under the bridge, along the river path and into the tunnel. He came back holding a wafer, a pale green wafer. "Otay ottenray eatmay," he uttered in a chant. The wafer turned into a chunk of old rotten meat, also pale green in color. He put the meat on the end of a long stick. "I'll be back in a minute. Be ready." He ran into the cave where the crab lurked.

"What's he doing?" Calypso was puzzled.

Yuri turned to Pre, "yes, what on earth was that?"

"The crab loves rotten meat," replied Pre. "The troll turned a wafer into the meat. We'd better keep an eye on him. With **those** kinds of tricks, no telling what he'll do."

They waited and then heard the faint shuffle of feet getting louder and louder. Rolly came backing out of the cave holding the meat on the stick. Following him was the giant winged crablike creature. The others backed away.

Rolly led the giant flying crab into the open. It had the greenish-red body of a crab with long white legs, giant reddish claws and wings and a large unicorn horn in the middle of its head. The hornlike protuberance could sting and render anyone unconscious if it managed to reach them. Yuri drew his sword preparing to fight the crab.

"Back, back. My sword will turn you to crab bisque. Prepare to die."

Calypso reached for her wand. "Oh, shoot, I forgot I lost it." Pre readied his staff for combat. As the crab surveyed its opponents, Yuri dashed around it and rushed into the cave. The crab realized it had been tricked, and turned to follow Yuri. As it did so, Calypso saw an opportunity.

"Quick, Pre, your staff," she yelled.

Pre went behind the crab and jabbed hard with his pointed staff at the back of the crab's neck where its weak spot was. The staff hit its mark with deadly accuracy. The crab stopped, screamed in a high pitched deathly shriek, went into a death spasm, swung around, and finally fell to the ground, rolled over, and died with its feet in the air.

"That takes care of it," declared Pre. "Let's drag it into the sea, where it really belongs."

Rolly, Pre, and Calypso dragged the huge heavy carcass of the dead crab to the shore and rolled it into the water.

"That should feed the Fins for some time," exclaimed Pre with satisfaction.

Yuri came rushing out of the cave holding Archie in his arms. "I think she's dead."

Pre stepped forward and held her pulse and felt her head. "No, she's unconscious, but her pulse is weak. She's still alive, but barely. No time to lose. Where's your sack?"

Yuri picked up the sack. Pre reached into the sack and pulled out some wafers. Rolly watched all of this activity with great interest. "Here, give her this," Pre continued. He gave Yuri a pink wafer. "But where's Murgi?"

"He's lying in the cave," Yuri said.

"Come on, Calypso," Pre yelled.

Pre and Calypso ran into the cave. Yuri held Archie in his arms while he put the pink wafer into her mouth.

"Oh, Archie. I'm sorry. I never should have left you. Please don't die." Finally Archie fluttered her eyes.

"Oh, Yuri, where am I?" she asked, sitting up. "What happened? Oh, I remember. That awful crab. Where is it?"

"Don't worry, Arch. It's dead. Oh, Archie, I thought you were a goner."

"So did I." Archie put her arms around Yuri and hugged him. Pre came rushing back out holding Murgi. He reached into the sack for another pink wafer. Calypso came out holding her wand.

"I found my wand," she shouted joyously.

"Never mind now about the wand. Here, give this to Murgi." Pre gave the pink wafer to Calypso, who held Murgi up and put the wafer in his mouth. "He'll be alright in a minute. Wow, that was close."

"What happened, Archie?" Yuri spoke quietly, his voice wavering and his brows furrowed.

"A huge claw grabbed me and dragged me into a tunnel. The last thing I remember was the huge stinger of the crab coming at me. I tried to get away but it got me in the back. I thought for sure that was it, Yuri," Archie shuddered.

"I'm glad we got to you in time. Where were you?"

"Oh, Yuri, what a sight. When we came above ground, I could see the remains of the old city. There are still sections towering high into the air, and some solar energy panels. Even now the city twinkles and soars in the air. They really did it. It's true. This must have been a magnificent city. I wish you could have seen it." Tears came to her eyes and she could not continue. Murgi began to stir and wake up.

"Let's get away from the lake and the open ground," shouted Pre to everyone. "I'll feel much safer down underground in the tunnels." He helped Murgi to his feet.

Murgi was still quite groggy and unsteady on his feet. "Uhhh. Where? Where are we? What happened?" Murgi mumbled slowly.

"On the other side of the lake," explained Calypso. "Are you all right, Murgi? I missed you."

"I'm alright I guess," he muttered. Murgi felt his sides and suddenly realized he had lost his axe as well as Calypso's wand, which he had put in his belt. "I lost my axe. And your wand. I was keeping it for you after you dropped it."

She produced her wand and showed it to him.

"Thank you for looking after it. I found it in there," Calypso pointed to the cave where she found her wand. She couldn't resist the temptation to be mischievous.

"Lost your axe, huh?" she teased. "Pretty careless." But he looked so forlorn she could not continue this suspense. She pulled out his axe. "You can thank Pre for this." She handed him the axe and he took it with reverence.

"My axe. I don't remember much. What happened?" Murgi inquired.

"It's a long story. We'll tell you on the way," Calypso answered quickly. "The important thing is that you're alright."

"Let's go," yelled Pre, as he entered the passageway with the river.

"Can I go with you?" asked Rolly.

"Of course," replied Yuri, "after helping save Archie and Murgi, you're a true friend." Yuri did not see the look of caution from Pre. Rolly had been eyeing Yuri's sack covetously, as Pre watched with mounting concern.

Pre just shrugged. "Well, alright, let's get away from here." Pre led them swiftly into the tunnel, staff in hand. He was followed by Yuri, with his backpack, and the sack in his hand. Calypso followed after, her precious wand in hand.

Archie moved slowly after them. She still had her backpack which had stayed on during the attack by the crab. Her face was cut up from being dragged unconscious through the tunnel. Her arm was bleeding from the crab's claw and her back ached but she struggled gamely onward.

Murgi staggered after her, his axe in hand. He was still very woozy from the stinger and looked a bit disheveled from the attack but he was not to be left behind.

Rolly was the last to enter the tunnel. He rubbed his hands together with glee and smiled. "I'm a true friend, he says." Rolly grinned widely as he ran after them.

As they moved through the tunnel the rumbling and shaking began again, this time much more violently than ever before. Small rocks and dirt fell to the floor.

After they left the shore area, Igor came paddling in slowly with the other boat and beached it next to their boat. He looked around at the cave and tunnel.

"Igor doesn't like Master anymore. Igor will call him Scarth, bad Scarth." Igor stood up straight with pride. "Igor will be brave. Scarth wants to steal the princess and the treasure, and kill the others. Igor won't let him. Igor will get there first and warn them." Igor quickly disappeared into the tunnel after the departing group.

Fat bulbous grotesque.

Pale green rotten meat. Crab smells.

Giant reddish claws.

TWELVE

The Giant Troll, the Cabbage Skunk, and the Ivy

The party of travelers had been moving swiftly through the narrow winding twisting passageways. *Pre must know these tunnels quite well,* Archie thought. *He seldom hesitates when we come to a fork in the maze of passages.*

The group strode resolutely through the passageways without a word spoken. With an increasing sense of urgency, they picked up their pace. The path continued on and on, but still Archie was convinced they were getting closer and closer to where they believed the princess was trapped. They all seemed to share that hope.

After many hours of travel, the pace slackened, and the group entered another cavern. In spite of her exhaustion, Archie entered first followed by Yuri, Pre, Calypso, Murgi, and Rolly. The first thing Archie noticed was the small river running through the cavern, and the huge amount of vines and moss growing all along the walls. They had emerged from an entryway carved out of a substance similar to slate, but she could see no other tunnel. The opening to one of two caves was covered with thick moss. The other was entirely covered by vines.

"I'm tired," Archie mumbled. "Can we rest?"

"Alright, but not for long," Pre replied.

"We can't go on," stated Yuri. "There's no passageway out of here."

"Maybe it's like that other cavern," Archie offered. "It's hidden. Look for a clue."

Pre ordered, "check the two caves. Murgi. Calypso."

Murgi went to the moss covered cave entrance and Calypso the vine covered one. She came back and shrugged her wings.

"Nothing there."

Murgi came dashing in, excited, holding a ball and some rocks. "Look what I found. There are more balls. They're all the same, but what do you think these rocks are?"

Yuri held the rocks for a moment. One of them had a sharp edge and the other had a groove. He fitted them together. "I think I know. It's a balance scale. Get the other balls." Murgi and Calypso retrieved the other round balls.

"Oh, I remember," Archie blurted. "The journal mentioned a magic ball."

"Oh, yes. There was a riddle about twelve balls and a balance scale," Yuri responded.

"One of them is either heavier or lighter. It's the magic ball," Archie added.

"And this scale is magic also. You can use it to weigh three times. After that it explodes if you try to use it again."

They looked at the scale and the twelve balls. No one wanted to test the magic. Then Murgi spoke up.

"I have it. I can find which is the magic ball."

"You, Murgi?" they answered with skepticism.

"We gnomes are not as dumb as you may think we are."

Calypso spoke softly, "we don't doubt you Murgi. But you could explain first."

Pre added, "yes, Murgi. Just in case. We'd all feel better knowing your idea first."

Murgi frowned but then explained in detail what would happen with the various options. They looked at Murgi.

Pre urged, "alright, Murgi. Makes sense. Let's do it."

Murgi took several balls and put the same number on each side. They did not balance. Then he took a different combination and did a second weighing. One side went down again. Then, finally, he did a third weighing, and held up one ball. He shouted with glee.

"This is the magic ball."

Calypso hugged him. "Congratulations, Murgi."

"Let's test it. Roll it against the wall," Pre ordered.

Murgi rolled the ball toward the opposite wall. The ball veered slightly and seemed to take its own course. It touched the wall and a large rock slid sideways revealing a passageway that was carved out of limestone.

"You did it," Yuri cried. He picked up the ball.

"Let's move on," Pre spoke. "We must be close to where the princess is trapped."

While this was going on, Rolly's eyes continued to be riveted on the sack that Yuri carried. He slid toward the Moss cave. Just before he disappeared into it, he popped a pale green wafer into his mouth.

Pre watched this activity carefully out of the corner of his eye. He saw Rolly swallow the wafer. When Rolly disappeared, he hurried over to Yuri.

"Yuri. Murgi," warned Pre sensing danger. "We may have trouble here. Rolly can't keep his eyes off your sack. He just popped one of those transmogrification wafers into his mouth and disappeared into that cave."

Before Pre could say anything else, there was a loud rumble and the ground shook. It wasn't like the earthquakes they'd been having, but something closer and more ominous. Suddenly a giant creature lumbered slowly out of the cave where Rolly had gone. With each footstep it took, the ground shook.

The monster was huge and towered over Yuri and Pre. Its massive gnarled head was hideous and misshapen, with bulbous nose and cheeks and eyes that could barely see through the rolls of fat hanging from its forehead. Its body and legs, with grotesque rolls of fat in layers hanging down, were equally ugly and misshapen.

The hideous creature held a giant club which it waved around erratically. It made low rumbling, roaring noises like the sound of a speeding oncoming locomotive.

Everyone pulled back to the sides of the cavern, as far as they could get. They raised their swords, staff, axe, and wands high as if to keep the monster at bay.

"Look out. It's a giant troll," yelled Murgi.

"It's Rolly," insisted Archie. "He was in that cave."

"It is," Pre answered. "I saw him take that green wafer."

The troll shuffled slowly to the center of the cavern. Yuri was near the Vine cave. He put the ball in his pocket, grabbed his sword, and held the sack in his other hand. The troll advanced toward Yuri with his club raised.

"Back, you beast," Yuri commanded, waving his sword.

"Run, Yuri. He wants the sack," screamed Pre.

"No. He'll taste my sword first. Prepare to die." He raised his sword even higher and took a step toward the troll as if to fight with the giant.

"Don't be foolish," Archie held up her hand as if to stop Yuri. "It's too big."

Just then, from behind the troll, another giant creature shuffled into the cavern.

"What's that?" yelled Archie.

"It's a cabbage skunk," explained Pre. "Stay clear."

It entered from the Moss entryway. The cabbage skunk was an ancient ancestor of both the skunk cabbage and the common skunk. It was very large, nearly as big as the troll. It had black and white stripes all over its body and legs, except for its head, which was bright yellow, like the new growth of the skunk cabbage. Its most powerful weapon was its overwhelming stench.

"What a stink." Yuri held his nose.

"Don't worry," Pre yelled. "It won't bother you if you stay out of its way."

The troll heard the skunk shuffle in and turned away from Yuri to face it. The skunk circled slightly to its left and the troll followed its movements. The odor of the cabbage skunk was so strong, however, that the troll could not stand the smell and backed slowly away from it in the direction of the Vine cave.

Unseen by the giant troll, a tall strange creature with dangling tendrils emerged, and stood behind the troll as it backed up.

"What on earth is that?" exclaimed Yuri.

"It looks like the rare walking ivy," answered Calypso.

The ivy was very tall, with a small pale green drooping head and tiny white eyes. It seemed to have small branches, or tendrils, coming out from every part of its body, with dark green ivy leaves on each. Two of the branches on the top had developed and looked like brown arms, and two others below were even more developed into dark brown legs that allowed it to shuffle slowly.

It stood upright and moved very slowly up behind the troll, wrapped its long tendrils around the troll and held it in a strong grip. Yuri, who had backed up against the wall of the cavern, decided to sheath his sword.

"You guys are doing fine without my help," he quipped.

The cabbage skunk continued to advance on the now helpless troll and the troll passed out from the strong stench. The ivy dragged the troll away into the Vine cave. The cabbage skunk shrugged and walked back into the cave it had come from. The astonished party moved to the center of the cavern.

"**What was that!?**" Archie pointed toward the cave where the cabbage skunk had disappeared. "You called it a cabbage skunk? And it did look like a cross between a skunk cabbage and a skunk, but how can that be?"

"Evolution's a strange thing," answered Pre. "It's probably an ancient ancestor of your two different species. This one's a plant eating mammal and lives close to the edge of our lake."

"And the other one, the one Calypso called a walking ivy?" she continued, pointing to the cave where the ivy had slowly dragged the helpless giant troll.

"Oh, that," he acknowledged and looked toward the cave where she indicated. "That one is carnivorous, a meat eating plant. I've only seen one other. They are very rare. They are an endangered species."

"Well, it didn't look in danger. The troll was the one in danger," Yuri smiled.

"Yuri, be serious. The ivy plant is almost extinct," responded Calypso.

Pre continued, "it has evolved also. When its habitat above ground was slowly destroyed, it gradually evolved into a walking carnivorous plant that lives below ground."

"Enough about all this evolution stuff!" Murgi interrupted. "Let's get going. Our princess is in peril. We must save her." He strode rapidly into the limestone passageway. The others followed without comment.

A short time later, Igor walked softly and slowly into the clearing, stopped in the middle, looked around and listened.

When Igor could no longer hear the footsteps, he heard an ominous sound from the Slate tunnel. He realized he was being followed. He slid into the Moss cave and waited.

An exhausted Scarth shuffled heavily into the cavern. He had tried his best to keep up with the footsteps he'd heard. He listened and entered the limestone tunnel. After he had disappeared, Igor came quietly out of his hiding place.

"I need to slow him down. It worked once. Maybe it will again. Then I'll follow **him.** That's a much better plan."

Igor used his staff to make loud footstep noises in the Slate passageway. His plan was to draw Scarth back into the cavern clearing and slow him up. Igor went back into his moss cave and waited.

The plan worked. Scarth soon returned and went into the Slate passage where he could hear the fading noises Igor had created. He came back into the cavern in a few moments, however, angrily shaking his fists, knowing he had been tricked. He looked around then returned to the limestone passageway. Igor came out of hiding and followed him.

Stinking cabbage skunk
Transmogrification. Troll.
Walking Ivy tendrils.

THIRTEEN

The Princess and the Gorgon

The party continued through the maze of underground passageways after leaving the shores of the lake. Since leaving the cavern and the encounter with the giant troll, they had traveled for several days. Archie had lost track of time in this seemingly endless underground world. The passageways twisted and turned, went down steeply for periods of time, and then abruptly started climbing again. She had no idea how far below ground she was, or how close to the side of the lake they were, but she could tell from the change in light that they were approaching another clearing or cavern.

The temperature was rising. In fact it was getting quite warm. She could hear sounds ahead that she had not heard before, a sort of bubbling sound. Was it a river, a running brook she heard? They were about to enter another clearing. She hoped they had finally reached the cave where the princess was held captive. Murgi was the first to emerge through the entryway, covered with thick moss and vines, nurtured by the heat and moisture. He halted when he spied the river of molten lava slicing diagonally across a corner of the cavern.

The cavern floor sloped from Murgi's left to right, and the lava slowly flowed from a wide crevice down the slope to the right and disappeared under the lower wall of the cavern. It spread out to a width of two or three meters. A small stream of gurgling water ran down the other side of the hot lava in parallel to it and disappeared into a cave. Murgi noticed another passage entryway near the spot where the lava entered. Rubble from the tunnel partially blocked the entrance. Most of the walls were covered with vines and moss growing from its many cracks and crevices.

Archie came running in behind Murgi and also pulled up abruptly when she saw the lava.

"Hello?" Murgi called, "anyone here?" He stood still and waited for a reply but there was none. No sound at all. Then, after a long delay, they heard a weak voice answer.

"Is someone out there? Hello?"

Archie realized the voice was coming from behind the wall of thorns and brambles.

"Princess, is that you? Behind the thorns?" Murgi called out and stood still, listening.

"Murgi, it's you. I'm trapped in here. I've been here a long time. Are you alone?"

"No, Archie's here. She's a friend, Princess, and Pre and the others are just behind us. Are you alright, Princess?"

"I'm very weak, Murgi, but I'm alright. Be careful. They'll be back soon."

"Who, my princess?"

"The heads."

"The heads, my lady?" Before she could answer, Pre rushed into the clearing, closely followed by Yuri and Calypso. Murgi continued, "here's Pre."

"Is our princess here?" Pre spoke through heavy gasps, trying to get his breath.

"Yes, she's in there, behind the thorns." Murgi pointed to the wall of thorns covering the cave entrance. "She's very weak."

"Princess?" Pre called hesitantly.

"Oh, Pre." Hearing the voice of Pre, the Princess was overjoyed and her voice gained a little strength. "I'm so glad you made it. Please get me out of here. I can't last much longer. I haven't eaten for a long time." Her voice trailed off with the effort.

"Yuri, quick," Pre said. "An orange wafer." Yuri reached into the sack and pulled out an orange wafer. "Can you throw it straight? Through the thorns?"

"Just watch." Yuri took a wafer, wound up as if he were a fastball pitcher and threw the wafer straight across the lava river through the wall of thorns. Archie marveled at how the wafer made it through the thick brambles.

"I've got it. I've got it," called Princess Mia. "Thank heavens." There was no time for the dainty manners of a princess. They could hear her devouring it. The party waited, and listened intently for her to speak again.

Finally Pre broke the silence. "Princess?"

"Pre, can you get me out of here?" She sounded a little stronger than before.

"We'll need help getting over the lava river," he answered as he contemplated the hot molten lava, "but we'll figure something out."

"Where is that wizard when you need him?" interjected Calypso.

"What are we going to do?" sighed Murgi.

"Be quiet a minute." Pre spoke sharply. He put his hand to his brow. "Let me think." Nothing was said for some time then the Princess continued very softly and slowly.

"Pre, be careful," she implored, "it'll be back any moment."

"It? What do you mean?" he asked in alarm.

"The beast. It never leaves for long. It's been guarding this cave for a very long time. It could return any minute."

"I'll take care of it," Yuri declared, "whatever it is." He drew his sword, turned in a full circle, waving his sword in the air at the imagined beast. Archie laughed.

"Yuri. Not again?" she giggled. "Put your sword away."

"Oh, be careful," Mia implored. "It's very dangerous. I think I hear it coming back."

They barely had time to consider her warning, when they heard a low rumbling shaking sound as a huge creature with two heads lumbered in from a passageway hidden by tangled vines.

"What is it?" shrieked Archie.

"The two-headed gorgon," screamed Calypso. "Oh, no."

The monstrous gorgon shuffled in on four short heavy legs supporting a grayish elongated body. Two long necks swayed back and forth. At first the two-headed gorgon looked confused. Each of its bobbing and swaying heads had red and black snakes in place of hair that twisted and slithered amongst each other as if to escape. The large black eyes were able to turn beholders to stone. They darted back and forth looking from one side of the cavern to the other. Each head roared, first one then the other then both together, as if they were talking to each other.

Pre quickly averted his gaze and screamed, "don't look at its eyes. Look away." Just in time, each one of the party turned away from the look of the gorgon's eyes.

"Why? What's wrong with looking at it?" yelled Archie.

"It will turn you to stone if you look into its eyes," answered Pre. "Follow me. We have to get away from here." Pre ran through the entryway of the passage partially blocked by rubble. "This goes upward to open ground." Archie and Yuri followed rapidly, jumping over the rubble.

"We'll be back soon, Princess," Murgi called as he followed Pre,. "to get you out."

"Take care of yourselves first, Murgi," responded Mia.

"We will, we will," Calypso cried out as she pushed Murgi. "Go, you big gnome." Calypso followed quickly after Murgi, not daring to look back.

"We have to go to the surface. We have no choice." Pre led them to the surface through the tunnel, with the gorgon lumbered slowly after them. Archie hated leaving the princess, still trapped. *I wonder how we'll ever get her out.*

Trapped behind brambles
Smoking hot lava river
Desperate. Alone.

FOURTEEN

The Flying Furies and the Gryphon

The party climbed up a steep grade in the last several hundred meters before emerging from the darkness of the winding underground passageway. As they reached open space each took a deep breath after running so fast. Pre exited first through an entry covered with scraggly thickets. He was followed in rapid order by Yuri, Archie, Calypso, and Murgi. They came out high on the side of the cliffs rimming the caldera that faced outward away from the lake.

The area was very open and sloped gradually downward toward a long valley below. They had a clear view but were very exposed from all directions. The razed landscape was bleak and bare, observed Archie, like the area she had seen before, but without any of the beauty of the destroyed city. The destruction and utter devastation was so complete that scarcely a bush or tree or any living thing seemed to exist. There were a few scattered rocks on the barren ground, which was devoid of life. She wondered what had happened to all the people and animals. Far in the distance she saw a dry river bed snaking through the valley. She mused: *I'll bet this was once a lush green landscape.*

Archie looked at Yuri, who had not been with her before high on the rim above ground. He appeared to have trouble adjusting to the light on the surface, but as he did, Archie could see he was stunned by the wasteland he saw before him.

"It's horrible, Archie. I had no idea."

The sky, on the other hand, realized Archie, did not have that stark look. It was different, with a soft kind of beauty. There were light clouds hovering in the distance. It had a light gray look blended in with a light blue color.

Archie looked around and saw several exits from the many passages coming up to the open ground. But there was no sign yet of the two-headed gorgon.

"Whew. That was close," sighed Pre. "Everyone here?"

"I think so." Yuri spoke up. He looked around at the members of the party. "Yes. What'll we do now?"

"Yuri, do you still have that mirror in your sack?" Pre continued. Yuri pulled it from the sack and showed Pre.

"Yes, here it is."

"Great. Keep it handy but put it away for now until we need it. I have an idea." Yuri put it in the sack, but sticking out, ready to grab.

"If the gorgon looks in the mirror," Archie asked "will it turn itself to stone?" Archie looked at Pre, then Calypso, hoping for an answer.

71

"No, I'm afraid not," piped up Calypso. "It's immune. A few **people** are immune to the sight of the gorgon's eyes as well, such as the princess."

"So what can we do with the mirror?" questioned Murgi.

"Protect us from its stare," answered Pre. "If we keep it in front of us to reflect its stare, we won't look at its eyes and turn to stone. My idea is to get close in and try to cut off a head or two with one of the swords," he explained. "I'm not sure it'll work, but it's worth a try."

"We have to do something." Murgi shook his head.

All of a sudden the ground began to shake and rumble. Slowly the two-headed gorgon shuffled out of the tunnel and roared twice. Everyone in the party immediately turned away from the look of the gorgon and headed away.

However, just at that moment, from every direction, bizarre flying creatures swooped in low to the ground and landed just in front of the party, surrounding them. They were ferocious winged creatures resembling a cross between a bat, bee, and bug.

They had the wings of a bat, the antennae and eyes and hairy body of a bee as well as a formidable stinger. Their long biting mouth parts resembled those of some sort of a bug such as a beetle. They made a loud clicking noise that was designed to terrify prey.

"Oh, no. The Flying Furies," Calypso cried out, "I was afraid of this."

"We're trapped," screamed Archie. "We're done for."

Pre and the others turned away from the Furies in terror. Unfortunately they turned back toward the gorgon, which looked straight at them and advanced. They all then made the fatal error of looking at the gorgon's eyes. Calypso yelled.

"Don't look." It was too late.

They all immediately turned to stone statues standing on the open ground. They froze motionless in whatever position they were in, in midstride with arms outstretched. The Furies, seeing that the group was now turned to stone, swept around and past them, and in their fury at being denied, viciously attacked the gorgon.

Some of them nipped and cut it's legs but many swarmed around the heads, biting and stinging all of its eyes until the beast could no longer see. Then it tried to escape away from the Furies into a tunnel.

They pursued it relentlessly, biting and slashing it until it was bleeding from many wounds. It tried desperately to reach the tunnel down which it could escape.

Suddenly a giant moth came up out of a passageway, and with its wings spread, descended upon the Furies. At first they tried to attack the body and legs of the moth but they were no match for the giant. It beat down upon them with its huge wings, scattering them with force and knocking them to the ground. They crawled away from the moth in several directions and rapidly flew away. The gorgon quietly slunk away, clumsily searching by smell for a tunnel, and disappeared. It was blind but was still alive.

The giant moth went over to Archie, touched her and dusted her with magic moth dust. It did the same with all the stone statues. Each of them began to return to life.

"Oh, what happened?" murmured Archie.

"You were turned to stone," replied the giant moth.

"Your voice," she went on. "You sound very much like someone we've met before."

"It's not surprising," acknowledged the giant but gentle creature.

"Tenty. You sound like Tenty."

"I **am** Tenty, my lady."

"Oh, Tenty," Archie cried out, "you saved us." The others gradually regained consciousness during this conversation.

"You helped **me** when it was most important. I'm glad to return the favor."

"What happened?" Murgi was groggy.

"We were turned to stone," answered Archie.

"Who's this?" Murgi was puzzled.

"It's Tenty. He saved us."

"How?" spoke up Yuri.

"Just a little magic moth dust," explained Tenty. "You see, amongst our kind, you could say I'm the prince of moths." He stopped for a moment and looked around. He spoke to the entire party. "What're you doing up here?"

"We were being chased," Murgi recalled "but I don't remember what happened."

"It's not safe," Tenty admonished, "I was lucky there were only a few Furies and I chased them away." He motioned toward the tunnel. "You should get below."

"Good idea." Yuri agreed and started moving toward the entrance. He stopped and turned. "What happened to the gorgon?"

"The Furies put out its eyes," replied Tenty. "It crawled away. I don't think it will harm anyone again."

"Aren't you coming with us?" asked Archie.

"No." Tenty spread his wings as if to fly away, "I have some business to attend to."

"Business?" inquired Archie. "We'd love to have you join us."

"I have to find a mate pretty soon and let nature takes its course. Otherwise I'd love to stay with you and help you complete your journey. Goodbye." Tenty moved in a direction away from the tunnel and the party, opened up his wings and flew away.

"Take care, Tenty," yelled Archie.

"Goodbye, Tenty," Calypso, Murgi, Pre, and Yuri spoke in unison, "and thank you." They followed Archie to the tunnel.

Tenty disappeared from view as the party went below. Archie led the way.

Fierce Flying Furies.

Lazarus turned into stone.

Magic moth dustings.

FIFTEEN

Saving The Princess

Archie sped down the winding, twisting passageway, followed closely by Yuri, Murgi, Calypso, and Pre. All was quiet in the cavern, except for the noise of the incessant bubbling of the flowing river of molten lava, and the faint sound of the small gurgling stream entering the cave. As Archie entered, she could see the steam rising slowly from the wide river. She squinted through the wall of thorns and saw the princess sitting quietly in the cave, head down. Mia looked up when she heard them dash in.

"Pre, is that you?" she called.

"Yes. Princess, are you alright?" he asked.

"Yes, I'm feeling much better. I'm so glad it's you. What happened? I thought the gorgon would get you." The Princess still spoke in a very tired, subdued voice. She had all but lost hope.

"It did. We were trapped between the gorgon and the Furies," he explained. "But we were very lucky."

"What do you mean?" she asked. "How did you escape!"

"The Furies got the gorgon's eyes, and an old friend came to our rescue." Pre felt now was no time for long explanations. "We're all alright now."

"I'm glad. I feared the worst. I feel so helpless here but I'm feeling better now that the beast is out of the way."

"What're we going to do?" queried Murgi. "We have to save the princess."

"I'm thinking," answered Pre.

There was a loud racket in the passageway entrance covered with moss and vines, and the party turned to look. Instinctively they all reached for swords and wands and axe and staff. They heard the clatter of footsteps, but not ordinary footsteps. These were heavy feet. The two WOOs came walking in, leading the Head Gryphon. The party put their weapons away. WOOTU carried a magic ball in its hand. The WOOs rhymed in unison.

"Have no fear.
  WOOs are here.
  Through the dangers, never lose.
  To the rescue come the WOOs."

"Well, look what we have here," smiled Calypso. "You weren't so brave when the shrooms attacked us."

Yuri pointed to the Gryphon. "What's that?"

"The Gryphon's on loan
  It's not one **we** own
  Yet it's free to roam
  But it has no home."

75

"Your rhymes are getting pretty pathetic," retorted Yuri.

"We've become so meek
  'Cause we're getting weak
  We have reached our peak
  Now it's food we seek."

"I'll give you each a food wafer." Yuri pulled a couple of wafers from his sack and gave each of them an orange wafer. Calypso noticed the ball in the hand of WOOTU.

"What's that?" Calypso pointed. "In your hand." WOOTU held the ball up so that everyone could see it, and turned to Pre.

"We heard your loud call
  Sam sent you the ball
  To knock down the wall
  To free one and all."

"So that's what Sam meant," Pre murmured, "he must have known about the lava river and the wall of thorns. Well, let's give it a try." Pre jumped on the back of the Gryphon, took the magic ball in one hand, and then asked the Gryphon to jump over the river of lava. The Gryphon spread its huge feathered wings, lifted into the air effortlessly, and floated over the hot smoking lava stream. It settled gently down on the other side of the river of lava, landing in front of the ivy wall on its clawed feet. Pre jumped down, and rolled the ball against the base of the wall of thorns. The magic ball parted the wall and created a hole large enough for Pre to go in to rescue the Princess.

Everyone cheered as he slipped inside to the weak Mia. Unfortunately, before he could return through the hole with her, the tough brambles grew at an enormous rate, closing the hole, trapping both of them inside. The cheering stopped immediately as they all realized a spell had been put on the wall. It too was magic. Everyone became silent until Calypso spoke out.

"Pre, the magic ball. Use it again," she yelled.

All waited until Pre found the magic ball inside the cave. He threw it against the base of the wall but nothing happened. The magic ball had lost its power.

"Nice idea, Calypso, but it doesn't work anymore. We've been trapped. I should have realized it wouldn't be this easy. I don't know what to do now."

Yuri remembered the other magic ball in his pocket, one Murgi had found to open a door in a previous cavern. He reached in and was about to pull out the ball when he hesitated. Perhaps this magic ball had also lost its power. Then Yuri felt a very sharp object and remembered what he had in his pocket.

"I have the solution." Yuri stepped forward. "Remember that wafer I threw?"

"Yes," Pre replied. "But what good will that do?"

"I have something better." Yuri pulled out the beautiful diamond he'd forgotten long ago to return to the box containing all the other diamonds. It was sharp, very sharp, and the hardest thing known. "Just watch this. And stand back, Pre," he cautioned.

Yuri wound up as much as he could and fired a fastball right at the center of the wall, where the thickest impenetrable section of the wall was located. The sharp diamond sliced completely through the thick twisted set of intertwined magic brambles. This time they did not grow back, so sharp and damaging was the cut.

Pre picked it up and sliced away until he had a hole big enough to walk through. Not only did the brambles not grow back but, mortally wounded, they began to shrink back away from the opening Pre created.

Pre picked up the very weak Mia in his arms and triumphantly carried her out. He put her gently on the ground. As he started to help her mount the Gryphon, she turned to him.

"Oh, Pre, you're my savior." Princess Mia put her arms around the neck of Pre and gave him a big long kiss. Suddenly there was a puff of smoke. Pre disappeared and Prince Peter appeared in his place.

"Mia, my darling. You've freed me at last from Scarth's spell." Prince Peter put his arms around Mia and returned a long lingering kiss. She put her arms around him as Peter lifted her up onto the back of the Gryphon and climbed up behind her. "Away," he yelled. The Gryphon leaped effortlessly over the wide river of lava. Peter lifted her off the Gryphon. She hugged him again, this time more tightly, lingering in his arms.

"Peter? Prince Peter, is it really you?" She snuggled against him.

"Yes, my princess, you're safe now." Peter held her.

"Oh, Peter," Mia lamented, "I've missed you so much." She gave him another long kiss. "What happened to you? You just disappeared."

"Scarth put a spell on me," Peter explained. "He turned me into a leprechaun, so he could have you for himself!"

"Never!" Mia declared adamantly. "I'd die first before I'd allow him to kiss me. It's you I've always wanted."

"Scarth thought, if he had you, he could rule the whole world." Peter held Mia tightly.

"And don't forget the treasure," Murgi piped up, "he wanted the treasure too. He wanted everything."

"Well, he can't have anything," Peter was vehement, "we'll see to that."

"Let's go find the Beetle," Mia shouted. "I don't want to stay another moment in this dungeon."

Encouraged by her strong forceful words, the WOOs went into the passageway, jumping over the rubble. They led the Gryphon behind them to the ground above.

"Let's go," Peter yelled out, but he was stopped by the sudden appearance of the dreaded Scarth, who emerged from the tunnel with the moss and vine covered entryway. He held his staff in his hand and surveyed them, all of whom were still there except for the WOOs, who had led the Gryphon away.

"Not so fast," he ordered. "I finally have you where I want you. I see you're finally free of my spell, Prince Peter. Well, that won't make any difference." Scarth raised his staff in a threatening gesture as he was about to put another spell on Peter and the rest of the party. Unseen by Scarth, Igor came running quietly in from the tunnel behind Scarth. He reached around and grabbed the staff.

"Not so fast yourself, Master Scarth. I'll be the master now." Igor raised Scarth's staff to put a spell on Scarth.

Peter intervened. "Hold it, Igor. Let's give him a fair chance." Peter turned to Yuri. "Yuri, give him your sword. What will it be, Scarth? Fight or run?" Yuri looked at Peter for a moment somewhat skeptically, but finally handed his sword to Scarth, who quickly took it. He looked around at the situation.

"Hmmm, one of my followers is blind, thanks to the Furies." He looked directly at Igor who looked boldly back at him, no longer afraid or obsequious. "Now one of them has become a traitor."

"You're the traitor," Peter charged. "Stand and fight." Scarth looked briefly back at the bramble tunnel.

"I have one ally left. Abersay, Igertay," he intoned. With that last incantation, the Saber-Toothed Tiger came out of the passageway with rubble in front. The Tiger let out a loud roar. Archie drew her sword and yelled to Peter.

"If you take care of him, I'll take care of this beast. It's time to show women can fight as well as men."

Archie charged the tiger and drove it back into the tunnel.

"I've got this beast under control," yelled Archie.

"Watch out, Peter," Yuri added, "Scarth is tricky."

Scarth took that opportunity to surprise Peter, and push him back almost into the lava river.

"Back, you leprechaun," Scarth sneered, "into the lava."

Scarth tried to push Peter into the lava river, but Peter reversed the position and had the upper hand briefly.

"You can try the taste of lava, you scum," Peter yelled.

The fighting was furious so the others got out of the way and flattened themselves against any safe wall space.

"Come on, Peter," urged Archie, "We can get them."

The battle seesawed back and forth. The tiger would charge Archie and try to push her back but she managed to keep the tiger in the tunnel entryway. Peter and Scarth had an even match in a duel in the center of the clearing.

78

"Easy for you," quipped Peter, "I have Scarth here."

Archie drove the tiger into the tunnel and it stayed there.

Yuri yelled to Archie, "Do you need some help?"

Suddenly the tiger roared and left through the passageway.

"I guess the tiger is the smartest of all," Archie said and sheathed her sword.

"I've lost my only ally," Scarth said, as he fought fiercely, pushing Peter back.

"Keep it up Peter," yelled Yuri, "You almost have him."

The battle between Scarth and Peter continued briefly, but suddenly Peter caught Scarth out of position and wounded him on the arm. It was severe enough to force Scarth back up to the passage entryway covered with moss and vines.

Without warning, the blind gorgon, which could still smell, reached in through the entrance, and with its two mouths wide open, grabbed Scarth in its jaws and dragged him away into the passageway. As he disappeared Scarth's screams of agony in his death throes were so horrible the others grimaced, closed their eyes, and covered their ears to block out the terrifying noise.

Igor had retreated to the safety of the passage with rubble in front. As he witnessed the end of Scarth, he rubbed his hands together in satisfaction, and unnoticed, disappeared into the tunnel from which he had come. All was quiet.

Archie smiled and turned to Peter. "What took you so long?" Peter smiled back and sheathed his sword.

"Well, now can we go to the Beetle?" interjected Murgi, "if you warriors are through with your competition."

Archie gave Murgi a playful squeeze with her arm. And then, before anyone realized it, there was Sam walking into the clearing. Calypso stepped forward.

"Look who's here? What took **you** so long?"

Sam smiled at her jest.

Peter continued the banter.

"Leave it to a wizard to show up after the action is over."

"I see you're free and feisty as ever. All of you." Sam looked around at the party, Peter and Mia, then Calypso and Murgi, then Archie and Yuri, and decided to offer some sort of explanation for where he had been. He turned back to Calypso. "I saved a few hundred people and creatures if you must know. I got them out of this area. You're the last around here. I wish we had more time to jest and trade words, but we must leave quickly." Sam looked around and noticed some faces were missing. "Where are the WOOs?"

"They left with the Gryphon before the battle," Murgi answered, "so then, what are **we** waiting for?"

Sam wrinkled his brows in concern and frowned.

"Hmmm! I saw the Gryphon up there but no WOOs." He pondered. "Oh well, they'll turn up I suppose. Let's go. You go find the Beetle. I'll catch up."

Mia led the party out of the cavern over the rubble into the tunnel. The rest of the party followed her. Sam was the last to leave. He took a different path, going through the other passageway. As they left the cavern, the ground shook and rumbled violently. Several rocks fell from the ceiling of the cavern, and there was a cracking sound as if the very rock walls were breaking apart. The ancient city of Montoba was slowly crumbling into ruins.

Seesaw battle scene.

Screams of Agony. Death Throes.

Savior. Redemption.

SIXTEEN

The Flying Beetle

The party climbed up out of the depressing and hot dungeon, as Mia had called it, and followed her up through the winding, twisting, passageway for twenty minutes. Suddenly Mia stopped and pointed out a smaller tunnel that took a slight downturn. Archie had not noticed it before when they ran from the gorgon. It looked as if it had been uncovered recently. Perhaps that was the reason they hadn't seen it before. This apparent recent activity did not faze Mia, who quickly followed this small passage down.

Archie noticed the walls were covered with moss, and smelled fresher than any other passageway they had travelled through. This sign of moisture instead of the dry dustier tunnels was a refreshing change. They had to stoop as they moved through the twisting passageway. Finally they went back up a very steep incline until they reached the top of the climb and out into open space.

This time they were almost at the top of the ridge and looked down upon the vast long lake that stretched for one hundred kilometers. They appeared to be approaching one end of it. They traveled along the ridge for another hour or so, and then dipped down again into a depression surrounded by steep cliffs on three sides. No vegetation grew here but the rocks were lavender-hued with silver streaks. *How lovely*, Archie thought.

In the middle of this small plateau sat a strange object. *Or was it a creature*, thought Archie. Suddenly she realized what it was from the drawings she had seen in the tablets and on the wall. It was the long sought after Flying Beetle. They must be at the treasure site. She was perplexed. What was the purpose of this creatue?

As she drew closer she could see the details of the object. Two tiny eyes followed her every movement. It shifted on its two hind feet. It was a living vehicle. A living thing that required food, or fuel, but it was a vehicle nonetheless. There was an opening in the front which was the entrance into the interior. There were two appendages in the front which looked amazingly like two human legs. She believed there were a pair of other such appendages in the back, but could not see clearly. A third set of appendages seemed more like arms and were on the sides pointing upward, unused at that moment. The roof or carapace or shell or whatever it was gave the appearance of a beetle, as did the beady little eyes. All in all, it looked like one but with human looking legs and arms. *An amazing sight*, thought Archie, *amazing!*

The Beetle sat in such a way that it was concealed from view, unless one stood on the cliffs directly above the plateau. Even the open side of the plateau was small enough so that a flying object would have to be close and looking directly into the depression in the cliffs. Alongside the edges of the plateau at the bottom of the sheer cliffs was a cave almost concealed by brambles and vines. The landscape was as austere and deserted as it was at the previous site when Archie emerged from a passageway to the ground above. Indeed, it seemed to be like that everywhere. At least there were clouds in the sky here, and the light was much brighter than it had been before.

Mia climbed down a steep winding path from the cliff ridges they had been following. She quickly reached the plateau followed by Peter, Archie, Calypso, Murgi, and Yuri. There were no signs of the WOOs.

Mia sighed in relief, "here we are." She waved her arms around indicating this was the site. "It looks as if no one's found this place in all this time. It seems to be undisturbed just as it was left."

"What happened to those mischievous WOOs?" Yuri looked around.

"We know they went to the other site because Sam saw the Gryphon there," Mia reasoned, "but they've disappeared." She shrugged. "They must have run off. I don't think they know how to get here."

"Where can they be then?" put in Peter, "I hope they're not lost."

"They're off getting into trouble, I'm sure." Archie threw her two cents worth in. "Maybe they went back to the cavern looking for us. Who knows!" She dismissed the subject. "I wouldn't worry too much. They'll turn up."

"My lady?" questioned Murgi. "Where's the treasure?"

"I don't know," Mia replied. "I tried to solve the riddle before, on my way here, but I couldn't figure it out. It tells where the treasure is. All I know is that it's not far from the ship. Sorry, Archie, we call the Beetle a ship."

"That's it," yelled Yuri, "the beetle is the ship in the riddle. I'll bet I can find the treasure."

Yuri walked to it, stood at the front and looked around. He noticed that its front was angled slightly and pointed directly toward the cave. He suddenly got an idea, and carefully paced off steps in the direction of the cave, and then disappeared into it slowly.

"What's he doing?" Peter was puzzled. "Where's he going?"

"I think he solved the riddle," Calypso replied. "He figured out the number of paces the ship captain takes on the pirate ship. That's where the treasure must be hidden."

"That's what the riddle's all about," Archie cried, "he did it!"

As they watched and waited, Yuri suddenly returned carrying a sack lightly over his shoulder. He was beaming.

"It's all the way back in that huge cave," he called excitedly, "sacks and sacks! What'll we do with all of it?"

"Thank heavens you found it," Mia answered. "Put as much as you can fit into the ship, please. Leave all the rest for the other people, if any are left that Sam missed. Murgi, will you help load it?"

"Of course, my lady." Murgi went off into the cave following Yuri, with Peter and Calypso trailing behind.

"Princess, what is the treasure?" queried Archie. "It doesn't seem to be heavy enough to be gold or silver."

"That's right," Mia agreed. "Gold and silver are of no particular value here. I would have added diamonds to that, but I've changed my mind, after Yuri's heroic efforts. They seem to be priceless." She smiled. "No, it's sacks and sacks of wafers we invented."

"Wafers? You mean like these?" Archie reached into the sack Yuri left with her when he went looking for the treasure. She pulled out a few different colored wafers.

"Yes, we have lots of food wafers." Mia held up an orange one. "You know about those. Yuri threw one of these through the thorns. Thank heavens. And we've lots of fuel wafers for the journey." She held up a tan wafer.

"Fuel wafers?" Archie was puzzled.

"The Beetle uses them as we use food wafers," Mia elaborated. "Each one lasts a year or more, perhaps even longer if it shuts down in hibernation." She reached in and brought out another wafer, a white one.

"What's that white one for?" Archie queried.

"This is our greatest invention." Mia held it up with reverence. "I guess you'd call it an anti-aging wafer."

"Anti-aging?"

"Yes, it slows down aging dramatically. For these long space voyages, we needed them. We live a very long time anyway but this is something special. Our bodies go into our own kind of long hibernation. We wake up periodically when our bodies run out of fuel."

"Did you say "we"?"

"Yes, Peter's going with me." Mia looked pleased and Archie smiled at this news.

During this conversation between Archie and Mia, the others had been walking back and forth between the cave and the ship, loading sacks and sacks into it. They finally stopped and stood at the entrance to the cave, resting and wiping their brows.

Mia and Archie put all the wafers back into the sack except for one that Archie held up: it was a yellow wafer.

"What's this yellow one for?" Archie inquired.

"Oh, that one's very special." Before Mia could answer, she was interrupted by Peter who walked over from the others. As Peter spoke, Archie absentmindedly put the yellow wafer into Yuri's backpack, left next to the sack.

"Well, that does it. We filled the Beetle."

"There are lots and lots of sacks still there," Yuri added.

"They're for Sam if he ever gets here," explained Mia.

Peter said to Mia. "Are you ready?"

"I guess so," she replied, "time to go?"

"Yes," he answered, "but first Murgi and I have something for Archie and Yuri." He looked around for the others. "Yuri? Murgi? Over here!"

Yuri and Murgi sauntered over from the cave entrance, followed discreetly by Calypso. Peter picked up the sack and handed it to Murgi. "You do the honors."

Murgi reached deep into the sack and appeared to be wresting something from the bottom of it. Finally he grabbed the object and slowly removed it from the sack.

"It's the box, Yuri," Archie shouted with joy. "They found it!"

Peter smiled. "Murgi and I wanted you to have it, to take it with you."

"The box that had the diamonds in it," exclaimed Yuri.

"They're all still there," Murgi assured him, and handed the box to him.

"Except for the one you took, and thank heavens you did," explained Peter. "You see, we've been aware that you found the box, but then you put it back in its hiding place. We realize how admirable that was, given the value placed on diamonds in your modern age."

Mia interjected, "They're of little use here, as you know."

Yuri opened the box reverently. "They're beautiful." After gazing for a moment at the diamonds, he handed the box to Archie.

"I am especially pleased to have the box. Thank you so much," added Archie.

"There's one other thing." Peter smiled.

"What's that?" asked Archie.

"You realize of course if you go back to the chamber where you found the box it won't be there any longer." His smile broadened.

She laughed. "I think I can understand that!" Pre never had this sense of humor, Archie said to herself, "and don't get me wrong. Yuri and I are also thankful to have the diamonds. They could help in so many ways."

Murgi offered, "perhaps you can use them to rebuild our beautiful city, especially the underground part."

"I'm sure we'll put them to good use, Murgi," Archie responded. She put the box in the backpack, and gave the pack to Yuri.

"It's time to get going," Mia spoke up.

Peter looked around. "Where's Sam? He should be here by now."

As if on cue, Sam came flying in above the cliffs on the back of the Gryphon, swooped down and landed next to the Beetle and the party.

"You called?" Sam smiled to Peter. No sooner had Sam alighted from the back of the Gryphon than the ground began to shake and rumble more violently than ever. Rocks came tumbling down the face of the cliffs landing dangerously near to the party.

"Watch out!" Yuri screamed, as he pushed Archie out of the way of a boulder rolling down the cliff. Another huge boulder almost smashed into the Beetle. Archie watched in astonishment as it nimbly stepped aside to avoid the rolling stone.

"Time to leave here," yelled Sam, "quickly now!"

"Sam," Mia interrupted him. "We left all the rest of the treasure for the people."

"We'll have to come back for it," Sam replied. "There's no time. Calypso. Murgi. You're going with me on the Gryphon. Far from here with the others."

"Yes, the sooner we get away from this place, the better," cried out Mia. "We don't have much time from the sound of it. The explosion's coming. Calypso! Murgi! Sam! When you find the WOOs, will you take them away from here as fast as you can?"

"Yes, my lady," responded Calypso and Murgi.

"I wouldn't worry about the WOOs," mused Sam. "They have a way of looking after themselves."

"Goodbye." Mia hugged each of the party quickly and headed for the Beetle. She turned back and called out, "and take care of yourselves." With that, Mia turned and climbed into the ship. Peter turned to Yuri and Archie.

"Those two wafers you saved? You should eat them." Peter gave everyone a hug, moved quickly after Mia, and climbed in. Everyone hugged everyone else.

Then Calypso and Murgi followed Sam to the Gryphon muttering to themselves.

"Those pesky WOOs," mumbled Murgi.

"Where can they be?" Calypso looked around.

"Those WOOs are smarter than you think!" mused Sam. "Don't be concerned."

Calypso and Murgi climbed onto the Gryphon. Sam clambered on behind them.

"Acalaphon! Gryphonala! Away," Sam yelled. The Gryphon lifted off slowly with the heavy weight on its back, flew up over the cliffs and away into the distance. As the Gryphon disappeared, the Flying Beetle sprang to life, and with a small whirring noise, lifted up and flew in circles high into the sky. It headed in the same general direction as the Gryphon. Archie followed the flights of the Gryphon and Beetle for a moment, and then turned to Yuri.

"Yuri, have you ever thought of what might have happened if we hadn't come here?"

"You mean what **did** happen," he countered. "Don't forget that. Good thing after all I ate that wafer. Perhaps by coming here we made a difference."

"You mean we changed the course of history?" she concluded. "Scarth would be on the Beetle now if we hadn't come here?"

"Probably," he shrugged. "Who can say? Anyway, let's get out of here before this thing blows up."

Archie and Yuri each took one of the gray wafers Archie had brought with them, and they held them in their hands. They looked at each other, closed their eyes, and this time, they popped the wafers into their mouths at the same time. There was a puff of smoke, a loud noise that no one heard, and Yuri and Archie disappeared from the plateau.

A strong wind came up, dark clouds rushed in, and it became very dark. If anyone had been there to listen, they would have been aware of an eerie silence descending upon the stark, desolate, and darkening landscape. The silence was broken by the first of several enormous earthquakes, which shook the ground as a giant troll might shake a rag doll. If there had been a single creature at that forsaken spot it would have been thrown violently to the ground.

The shaking was followed by the first of a series of violent explosions that roared and echoed from cliff to cliff. The lake itself and what was left of the mountain exploded in deafening cataclysmic waves of sounds. Plumes of fire and smoke and ash erupted in numerous spots across the entire length of the lake and the cliffs around. The explosions were of apocalyptic proportions, probably never seen then, and certainly never seen since – at least not yet. The survival of mankind was hanging by a thin thread.

Evacuation.

Explode. Apocalyptic.

Supervolcano.

SEVENTEEN

Back Home at Yale
January, 2037

Archie and Yuri reappeared in Archie's room in the exact same spots they were in when they took the first pair of wafers. Yuri dumped the backpacks on the floor, as they each dropped heavily into a chair.

"No one will believe us if we try to tell them what just happened and where we've been," Yuri spoke softly. He was clearly dejected after so many highs and lows during this extraordinary adventure.

"They might," Archie responded, without conviction.

"They'll just ridicule us. They'll think we're crazy."

"Maybe it's best, for the time being, if we don't say anything. Let's not discuss it with anyone," Archie paused, "not even Andre."

"Alright," agreed Yuri. "Anyway, we don't have any evidence to support our story."

"What about the box of diamonds?"

"That will just get us in trouble. We have no way to prove how we got them. They'll say we held back the box from Andre because of the diamonds or something like that." They sat silently.

"Then we'll just have to find more evidence, won't we?" she said softly and firmly.

Archie and Yuri just sat there for a moment, not knowing what to say or do next. Then the phone rang. Archie answered it. She whispered to Yuri. "It's Andre." She listened politely for a minute, then answered "alright" and hung up. She looked stunned.

"What was that all about?" asked Yuri.

"He wants to meet with me at the library in the morning. He just got the report of the radiocarbon test. He says it's astounding news and says we must find a way to go back."

"How can that be? That was weeks ago. He just got the report?" Yuri suddenly looked at the digital clock. "Archie, look. Time stopped while we were gone. It's only a few minutes from the time we left." They were dumbfounded.

"So?" she challenged. "Maybe it was all a dream? Is that what you think?" She dared him to say it was just a mirage.

"For both of us?" he responded. "No, Arch, it couldn't have been. But you've heard of the work on parallel universes? Maybe we just dropped into a parallel timeframe, but remembered everything."

"I think we need a break from this for a while. People may think we're crazy if we mention any of this. I don't want to feel I'm crazy too. It happened.

We know it. We have the proof. That's all that matters to me. But I'm not sure what to do about it yet."

"Alright, Arch, whatever you say. Let's just go about our business for now."

"I'll meet with Andre and hear what he has to say," she said, which ended the discussion for both of them.

When she met with Andre, he did all the talking. He would make arrangements to go back to the dig, and would let her know when it was set up. It would take several weeks to arrange. Both she and Yuri would go. They would try to find the passageway she had explored, try to find the box and the diamonds, and go from there. She didn't know what to say, so she said nothing.

And how could she let Andre know that it would be a waste of time to return to look for the box? She had to find a solution to this dilemma. Soon!

Archie and Yuri spent the next several weeks in different ways. Archie spent most of her time, when she was not in class, writing in her journal, recording everything she could remember. She felt the least she could do was to document their journey while it was fresh in her mind. Yuri went about his business, spending his time, when he was not in class, at the telescope, tracking his discovery in space.

They agreed not to discuss this strange improbable adventure with anyone. For safekeeping, they separated the box and the diamonds. Yuri locked the diamonds in a special safe deposit box. Archie kept the box.

One momentous day, while Archie was writing, she thought of a solution to the dilemma about the box. She had smuggled out the wafers. She would smuggle in the box. On her next trip to the library, she put the box with the tablets, as a "gift" to Andre, she reasoned. She was not sure what he would think, but she would have an explanation when Andre discovered it. Perhaps she would say it must have been put into her pack and they forgot about it. She wasn't sure that would work but she would keep thinking of a better one. As she left the library, she decided to drop in to Yuri's room and see how he was doing. She tossed her backpack on the floor next to his.

He looked up. "Hi, Arch." She stared expectantly.

"No, I still don't know," he said in response to her quizzical look.

She sat down heavily.

"We've been back many weeks," she challenged him. "You still can't fix the time it'll arrive in the atmosphere?"

"Archie, I can fix the time, but the whole thing doesn't make sense."

"What do you mean?" she pressed him.

"You remember, when we came back here time hadn't changed," he reminded her, "even though we were gone for months?" He paused.

"Everything was exactly the same as when we left, right? The clock hadn't changed."

"Yes, yes, how could I forget," she snapped, "so what's your point?"

"Archie, time didn't stop for that object in space." He stopped for a moment and then resumed. He spoke emphatically. "I **know** when it should arrive."

"When?" She challenged him again.

"In seventeen days."

"From now? Amazing! Are you sure?"

"Yes, February twenty sixth," he answered with authority, as if there were no doubt of that, "but how could time keep moving for the object, and not for us?"

"Well, you said it," she shrugged, "a different time space?" But Yuri still looked worried. "There's something else you're not telling me, isn't there?"

"Archie," he murmured quietly, "I'm not sure you're going to believe me."

"Try me," she demanded defiantly.

"It looks like the Flying Beetle." Now he really had her full attention. She jumped up and tossed down her journal. She started to run out.

"Is the telescope set up?" she yelled. "Can I look at it?"

"Go ahead. Tell me what you think." She ran out the door. While she was gone, Yuri looked at some notes he had made. He then reached absentmindedly into his backpack and felt the magic ball. He pulled it out and looked at it. Then he shook his head and put the ball back into the backpack on the floor. As he did so he felt something strange in there, and pulled out the yellow wafer. He held it up and was looking at it when Archie came running in.

"Sure looks like it," she panted. "Do you suppose it is? Is it possible they're still on it? Still alive?"

"We'll find out soon enough," he replied, "someone or something is making it change direction as it gets closer," Yuri continued, "Archie?" he said softly.

"Yes?"

"What's this?" He held up the wafer. "A yellow wafer? I've never seen this before. I found it in my backpack."

"Yes. It's a special wafer," she acknowledged. "Mia was just about to tell me about it when we were interrupted. I wonder what it's for?"

"Well, there's one way to find out." Yuri pretended to put it in his mouth. Archie leaped toward him and grabbed his arm.

"Yuri, no!"

He laughed and put it down on the table. Then he put his arm around her.

"Just kidding, Archie," he paused for a moment and spoke softly. "Archie?"

"Yes?" Archie whispered, put her arm around him and hugged him closely.

"What do you suppose ever happened to those WOOs?" he pondered.

"I've wondered about that too," she reflected, "they were very clever, you know. Maybe…?" She stopped and looked into the sky. Then she shrugged.

Yuri followed her gaze. Archie reached up and gave him a long kiss. They hugged each other tightly as they stared at the approaching object. Seventeen more days, she pondered, and their adventure will have gone full circle. She shivered in Yuri's strong arms.

Spaceship returning.

A parallel universe?

The seventeenth day.

The End.

APPENDIX A

The Eggs In The Basket Riddle

A peasant woman had a basket of eggs to sell. In rapid succession she sold half of the eggs and half an egg more to the first customer, half of the remaining eggs and half an egg more to the second, and finally, half of the remaining eggs and half an egg more to the last customer. He was the last because all the eggs were sold. No eggs were broken.

How many eggs were in the basket to start with?

Answer

Seven – Half of these and half of an egg is 4, leaving 3. Half of these and ½ an egg more is 2, leaving 1, and ½ of these and ½ an egg more is 1, leaving none.

The Monkey and The Coconuts Riddle

Three men spent the day gathering coconuts and putting them in a large pile at the end of the day. They went to sleep with the intention of splitting them equally the next morning.

In the middle of the night one of them woke up and split the pile in three. There was one left over and he threw it to a monkey sitting in a tree. He hid one pile, put the two remaining piles together and went back to sleep. A second man did the same: split the remaining pile into thirds. One was left over and he gave it to the monkey. He hid one pile and put the other two piles back together. The third woke up and thought the pile was smaller than he remembered but split it into thirds and hid one pile, giving a left over coconut to the monkey.

In the morning the three woke up and all noticed how small the pile was but said nothing. They split it in thirds and one was left over, which they gave to the monkey. The monkey, thankful for the four coconuts which it hid, also said nothing. One by one, unnoticed by anyone but the monkey, each took away their third and their own hidden pile. No one but the monkey was the wiser.

Being very wise yourself, tell us:

What is the smallest number of coconuts that could have been in the original large pile?

Answer

Seventy-nine. Splitting those into three each of 26 and one for the monkey leaves 52. After splitting those there would be 34 left. Splitting those leaves 22 and finally they split down to 7 each. The first one gets 33, the second one gets 24, the third gets 18 and the monkey gets 4, for a total of 79.

To prove it's the smallest work backwards with lower numbers.
1->4->7->end
2->7->end
3->10->16->25->end but close
4->13->end
5->16->25
6->19->end
7->22->34->52->79

APPENDIX C-1

The Pirate Chief's Riddle

In the seas around Sumatra, pirates lurked everywhere, hidden in coves and bays, preying on large ships containing cargo, sometimes including many passengers. Often the pirates would seek ransom for either the cargo or the passengers, or both. One time, when a small pirate ship captured a large merchant ship, the pirate chief made an offer to the captain of the merchant ship that might save his life.

The pirate chief said he could not keep all the passengers and ordered his crew to line up all 500 of them in a straight line from the bow of the deck to the stern, and ordered his first mate to stand in the first position. He told the captain he would give him a chance to pick his own place in line after he told him what he was about to do.

In a tankard were the numbers from 2 to 7. After the captain stood in line, the pirate would pick one of those numbers at random. If the number were two he would throw overboard every 2nd person and stop. But if the number were three then he would toss overboard every 3rd, and then go back and throw over every 2nd of the remaining ones. The higher the number the more times he would go through the line. If seven he would throw over every 7th, then every 6th of the remainder, then every 5th down to 2.

The captain could not stand in first position and did not know which number would be picked. He stood behind the first mate and thought for a moment. Then he slowly paced off positions in line starting with the first mate until he took a place in line where he was completely safe no matter what number the pirate chief picked. The pirate chief smiled since he realized this captain was a very smart one. They became friends for life based on mutual respect, even though they continued to remain in different walks of life.

If you were the captain, what position would you take? How many paces did he take?

Answer

The product of the common factors of all numbers plus 1 is the only safe spot. 2x2x3x5x7+1=421. Other than position 1, which is not available, the best place to keep from being picked is to stand behind a person that will **always** be selected no matter what number is selected and to continue to stand behind one that will be selected.

If number 7 then 60 people are selected in front of you then 60 more until 360 are taken.
If 6 then 70 each time for total of 350. If 5 then 84 for total of 328. If 4 then 105 for total of 315. If 3 then 140 for total of 280 and finally, if 2 then 210. You are safe no other place!

APPENDIX D

The Twelve Balls Riddle

Lying in a pile are twelve identical spherical balls. They look the same, they appear to be the same size, but one is different. One is a very special magic ball that does not weigh the same as the others. It is either heavier or lighter but not the same weight. Near the pile is also a very special scale that one can use only three times for an accurate weighing. The magic ball can be used to perform many magic tricks but the other eleven balls are very dangerous. Any attempt to use them can cause enormous destruction and death.

In your mission it is very important to identify the magic ball and to do so using the magic scale only three times. The scale is a balance scale where one can put a number of balls on either side to see if they balance, or if one side is heavier or lighter. Attempting to use the scale a fourth time will cause its destruction. Using the scale for three and only three times, how would you weigh the twelve balls to determine which is the magic ball?

Answer

Weigh four on each side. (Call them 1-4 and 5-8. Call the other 4 9-12)

If they balance, weigh 3 of the other 4 (9 and 10 on one side and 11 on the other side) plus 1 of the other 8 (2 each side). If they balance, weigh the remaining ball (12) against any to see if it is heavier or lighter. Otherwise weigh 9 and 10 against each other. If they balance and were heavier, then 11 is lighter. Otherwise 11 is heavier. If 9 and 10 were heavier and 9 is heavier, then 9 is the ball; otherwise 10 is lighter. If 9 and 10 were lighter and 9 is lighter then 9 is the ball; otherwise 10 is heavier.

If 1-4 and 5-8 do not balance, then weigh 1 plus 6-8 against 5 plus 9-11. If 1-4 was heavier and 1 plus 6-8 are heavier, then either 1 is heavier or 5 is lighter. Weigh 1 against any but 5. Similarly, if 1-4 is lighter and 1 plus 6-8 is lighter than either 1 is lighter or 5 is heavier. Weigh 1 against any but 5.

If 1-4 was heavier and 1 plus 6-8 was lighter or if 1-4 was lighter and 1 plus 6-8 was heavier, then it is one of 6-8 (lighter or heavier, resp.). Weigh 6 against 7. If they balance then 8 is lighter or heavier, resp. If 6-8 lighter and 6 lighter, then 6 otherwise 7. If 6-8 heavier and 6 heavier, then 6 otherwise 7.

If 1 plus 6-8 balance against 5 plus 9-11 then it is one of 2-4. Weigh 2 against 3. Follow same logic as above to decide if 2, 3 or 4 and heavier or lighter.

APPENDIX E

WAFERS Used

Gray (Time - Transporting)
Orange (Food)
Pink (Anti-venom)
Pale Green (Transmogrification)
Tan (Fuel)
White (Ageing)
Yellow (?)

APPENDIX F: HAIKU

Carboniferous
Hieroglyphic mystery
Antiquity runes.

Booms and puffs of smoke
Transporting magic wafers
Ancient times revealed.

Diaphanous wings
Shimmering gossamer dress
Dainty pointed shoes.

Vast splendid city.
Memories: destruction, death.
Weak, starving, cave-trapped.

Phosphorescence. Elves.
Magic mirror, vision, fear.
Rumbling. Shaking. Rocks.

Cocoon encasing.
It's the season for change, but
Butterfly or moth?

Ugly shrooms attack.
By flowing wizard rescued.
Steaming spicy soup.

High soaring towers
Twinkling glittering vision.
Cafes. Cabarets.

Tentacles grasping
Thunderous waves spraying water
Surging from the deep.

Fertile Green Valley
Devastated, destroyed.
Dark Continent Bound.

Fat bulbous grotesque.
Pale green rotten meat. Crab smells.

Giant reddish claws.

Stinking cabbage skunk
Transmogrification. Troll.
Walking Ivy tendrils.

Trapped behind brambles
Smoking hot lava river
Desperate. Alone.

Fierce Flying Furies.
Lazarus turned into stone.
Magic moth dustings.

Seesaw battle scene.
Screams of Agony. Death Throes.
Savior. Redemption.

Evacuation.
Explode. Apocalyptic.
Supervolcano

Spaceship returning.
A parallel universe?
The seventeenth day.

www.ingramcontent.com/pod-product-compliance
Lightning Source LLC
Chambersburg PA
CBHW030601130626
46552CB00006B/2628

* 9 780099 138971 1 *